'You're On!'

'You're On!'

How to Develop Great Media Skills for TV, Radio and the Internet

Alec Sabin

Viva Books
New Delhi | Mumbai | Chennai | Kolkata
Bengaluru | Hyderabad | Kochi | Guwahati

First Indian Edition 2010
Reprinted 2013

VIVA BOOKS PRIVATE LIMITED

- 4737/23 Ansari Road, Daryaganj, New Delhi 110 002
  E-mail: vivadelhi@vivagroupindia.net, Tel. 42242200
- 76, Service Industries, Shirvane, Sector 1, Nerul, Navi Mumbai 400 706
  E-mail: vivamumbai@vivagroupindia.net, Tel. 27721273, 27721274
- Jamals Fazal Chambers, 26 Greams Road, Chennai 600 006
  E-mail: vivachennai@vivagroupindia.net, Tel. 28290304, 28294241
- B-103, Jindal Towers, 21/1A/3 Darga Road, Kolkata 700 017
  E-mail: vivakolkata@vivagroupindia.net, Tel. 22836381, 22816713
- 7, Sovereign Park Apartments, 56-58, K. R. Road, Basavanagudi, Bengaluru 560 004
  E-mail: vivabangalore@vivagroupindia.net, Tel. 26607409, 26607410
- 101-102 Mughal Marc Apartments, 3-4-637 to 641, Narayanguda, Hyderabad 500 029
  E-mail: vivahyderabad@vivagroupindia.net, Tel. 27564481, 27564482
- Beevi Towers, First Floor, SRM Road, Kaloor, Kochi 682 018, Kerala
  E-mail: vivakochi@vivagroupindia.net, Tel: 0484-2403055, 2403056
- 232, GNB Road, Beside UCO Bank, Silpukhuri, Guwahati 781 003
  E-mail: vivaguwahati@vivagroupindia.net, Tel: 0361-2666386

www.vivagroupindia.com

Published by arrangement with
How to Books
Spring Hill House, Spring Hill Road
Begbroke, Oxford OX5 1RX,
United Kingdom

NOTE: The material contained in this book is set out in good faith for general guidance and no liability can be accepted for loss or expense incurred as a result of relying in particular circumstances on statements made in the book. The laws and regulations are complex and liable to change, and readers should check the current position with the relevant authorited before making personal arrangements.

ISBN : 978-81-309-1467-1

Published by Vinod Vasishtha for Viva Books Private Limited, 4737/23, Ansari Road, New Delhi-110 002. Printed and bound by Raj Press, R-3, Inderpuri, New Delhi - 110 012.

M0000

For Pippa

Contents

Acknowledgements

Philippa Hurd for invaluable professional editorial advice. I am indebted to her for all the support and valuable time she has given me on this project.

I am grateful to the following:

- Andrew Burroughs for valuable information and advice on TV journalism and production
- Simon Griffin and Kevin Oliver for useful TV and technical advice and information
- Fiona Macdonald for valuable professional discussion and suggestions
- Andrew Walker for advice and contacts on TV.

My thanks also to:

- Elizabeth Estensen for her insights into TV feature programme interviews
- Rebecca Sabin for editorial contributions.

A lot of the problems and their solutions have come from my many trainees including:

- Journalists and staff at the BBC
- Students at The City Lit, London
- Actors and students at the Actors Centre, London
- Corporate and private clients.

Introduction

WHO IS THIS BOOK FOR?

People who want presentation training do so for a variety of reasons. Some want to be professional presenters, and I certainly address myself to those who want a career in front of the camera or microphone. But I also see this book as being for people from a range of working environments, with differing professional abilities, who commonly have a desire or need to improve their presentation skills.

They may want help dealing with media professionals – how to be an effective interviewee. Experts and academics often want tips when asked to appear as guests on radio or TV. They want to know how they can best get their ideas and information across to a more general audience. Writers and print journalists may want to move into radio or television with a need to master another medium. They may want to learn effective podcasting. Media and journalism students as well as those usually behind the camera and microphone can find out what it is like in front of them. Producers, directors and editors often ask me how to get the best out of their presenters. Actors and other performers may want the challenge to be themselves, for a change, in front of an audience. All kinds of professionals, corporate and management, may want help with making speeches or presentations to groups of colleagues or clients.

There is something here for all these people and though this book focusses on the electronic media, where the audience is not physically in front of the presenter, the techniques discussed will be useful for any presentation, since the principles involved generally apply to all presentation.

THE EXCHANGE

In my experience as a voice and presentation trainer I have found that when the best work is being done both parties are learning something – both my trainee(s) and myself. There is an exchange. It is true that some of my trainees may be experienced journalists with sophisticated ideas and a good deal of information about interesting parts of the world. I have worked with journalists from all over the world: Eastern Europe, Russia, Central Asia, Iran, the Arab world, China, South East Asia, and many countries in South America and Africa, and obviously there is much for me to learn. But even when I am working with beginners or corporate non-media clients what needs to happen is for them to give me something.

As a trainer I become a professional listener, and when asked, as I sometimes am, to judge someone's performance on air, I usually say that I do not 'do' judge: I am a facilitator. My role, as audience, is to ask 'am I being served?' and if not, why not; and I then try to look at ways, with my trainee, to correct that. But they are the judge of their own presentation.

This book therefore is for those with something to give. You may not know exactly what that is. It may need to be worked on, thought about, written, corrected. But the desire to express it is already there. I can help you get that across through the electronic media. The presentation of your material is what concerns me, and should concern you. Here are some ideas about how you can improve your performance.

Back to basics 1

WHAT IS PRESENTATION?

I think it is useful to start with an analysis of what we usually mean by presentation to look for some essential elements that will help us improve performance. What is going on when someone is 'presenting'? What are they doing? Offering, showing, exhibiting, giving, bringing (to the attention of), introducing? All these, and more. Certain activities surely involve presentation and/or associated skills: making a case in the courtroom or debating chamber for instance; social etiquette – introducing someone; teaching; acting and comedy; even giving an award in recognition of achievement. What then do these have in common? There are three things which are relevant to the business at hand:

- A form or formality
- People – the public
- The transfer of something to one or many others

What is useful about such an analysis is that we can instantly recognise these concepts in TV and radio presentation. When you present on the media you offer, you show, you bring, you give and introduce. The form is the medium, the public are involved, and it is a transfer of information from presenter to the audience.

Who uses presentation skills?

Almost everyone. Presentation skills are surely a necessary part of human communication and language. This would include therefore conversation. To speak is to present. And it is interesting to note before we move away from this reductive analysis, that conversation is the model I use for trainee presenters and their guests to encourage them to adopt the same register to engage their audience: I ask them to imagine they are having a conversation with their viewers and listeners. In so doing they are employing universally recognisable skills most of us started learning at our mother's knee.

Jumping ahead to professional uses of these skills, beyond chatting on the phone, telling jokes, even 'doing presentations' at work or college, let us look at the defining elements useful for media presentation. Who, apart from TV and radio presenters and their guests, learn and use these skills?

Comics, actors, teachers, politicians, barristers, salespeople and journalists to name a few, surely use them.

I often ask new trainees whether they have previous experience of presentation and I would include the work of any of these worthy professionals as valid and useful experience. However most of the professional activities of these people involve something in addition to merely putting over information. So while it is useful for a presenter to be able to persuade, amuse, entertain, sell and teach, and these people make able on-screen/on-mic performers, these skills are not necessary ones for media presentation.

I say this to point out the problems some of these professionals face as media presenters. Actors, for instance, ask me whom I want them to be when they read the news, or promote a programme. I usually answer, 'how about yourself?' This can be met with a frown.

I knew a voice-over artist used to making commercials who when he read the news sounded as if he were selling something. Salespeople may do the same, although if they're presenting on a shopping channel their skills may come in handy. A comic may feel the need to find something funny to say when it is not appropriate; a politician to win over his or her audience.

They are all doing something additional, which in media presentation is not only unnecessary it may be counter-productive. So when I ask them to *merely* put over the information, they realise that there is a skill involved which they may have taken for granted.

Theoretical study

It is perhaps worth pointing out here that a discussion of presentation, like a discussion of comedy, will not on its own help you be a better practitioner of it. There are no degrees in it even if (happily) there are parts of media courses which include presentation and voice training. But in searching for definition perhaps we can learn something about what it is not and how we should handle the ambition to become a better presenter and media performer.

Presence

There is a useful part of presentation which is simply presence: being there; occupying space; inhabiting it; belonging in front of the mic or camera. Your audience will react to you before you have told them anything. On television especially when they can size up your appearance, but even on radio in the short time you take to say: 'hello, I'm Alec Sabin, welcome to this week's programme...etc' the audience will have had some thoughts about you. Focussing on this can put you at a disadvantage since you will feel judged. But it is important to acknowledge it. Keep with your material (script or ad-lib) in the present moment. This will help you to think on your feet and not allow distractions to compromise your concentration.

The bad side of 'presence' is vacuity: that you are present, the lights are on, but no one is home. Actors acknowledge this. Sometimes they refer to 'sending the beard on' or 'phoning it in' – derogatory terms denoting lack of involvement in their work. This assumes the audience will 'get' the character through facial hair alone, or the text without real commitment from the actor, their vacuous presence being all that is necessary.

Focus of attention

We will see later what the qualities of *good* presentation are, but we can already define three necessary elements of any presentation:

- The presenter
- The presented to – the audience
- That which is presented – the material

It is as well to define the essentials but I offer them also to highlight something important: focus of attention. The presenter can choose to focus on any of these three, and the audience on two of them.

However it is important that the presenter focus on only two of them: the audience and the material. The audience should focus on only one of them: the material. This cuts out the presenter. Let's see what this means in practice.

The presenter

It is perverse perhaps to suggest that the presenter should be ignored, in favour of the audience and material; but the presenter's expertise will paradoxically be evident and appreciated all the more for the lack of distraction by unnecessary signature.

Such is the audience's lack of the need to be reminded of the existence of the presenter, that I suggest the best presentation often happens when none seems to be going on. This then can concentrate the audience's mind on what is being presented to them. If as a listener you are absorbed in something on the radio in your car, perhaps you only become aware of listening to the radio at all when you reach your destination and need to switch off and leave the car. Likewise, you only become aware of the radio functioning when it needs tuning (rarer now with automatic tuning in the car). You also may only become aware of the presenter if and when he or she makes a mistake.

In that chain of communication in radio presentation –

from ideas/information – in the presenter's brain – to voice – to microphone in a radio studio – through control room and transmission – to aerial – to receiver – to the ear – and brain of the listener –

ideally the listener should be aware of nothing other than the ideas or information being imparted: the material, and not all those other links between. It should be a purely intellectual process: a flow of ideas from the presenter's brain to the listener's. And awareness of the presenter should be as negligible as awareness of the aerial on the top of the car, although both are necessary to the reception of those ideas and information.

The presented to – the audience

Although the audience does not need to focus on the presenter, the inverse is not true. In order for the audience to focus on your material you will need to engage them. And before engagement comes awareness. Even though they are not visible to you, you can effect awareness of them by developing a kind of imaginary personal antenna which will tell you when you are getting your material across to them and, more importantly, when you are not doing that. This will enable you to fine tune your skills in the process of becoming a good communicator. If your audience were visible you could *see* them listening to you or not.

In some cases the presenter/audience relationship should be like a one-on-one conversation, where there is interaction. Obviously there is a leap of imagination involved here, but it is an important one. Think about the situation when you are talking to someone who has stopped listening to you – their eyes have glazed over. How does that feel? What do you do about it? Do you carry on? Do you jolt them into listening to you? You need to reconnect with them for the process of communication to continue. You can have the same feeling in broadcasting. There will be times when you feel you have lost your audience. How do you get them back?

Some presenters and broadcasters like to imagine they are talking to one particular person whom they have in their mind's eye. It is often someone they know – a friend or relative. There are advantages and disadvantages to this technique, but it highlights the need that many professionals feel about engaging their audience which they rightly recognise to be of utmost importance. There will be more on this technique in Chapter 4.

That which is presented – the material

At Speakers' Corner in Hyde Park in London, I once saw someone on a soap box saying to his admittedly rather small but nevertheless hardy audience that he had nothing to say to them, that he didn't know why they were standing there listening to him and wouldn't they be better off going to listen to someone else. They stayed, though, and he kept on talking, saying more or less the same thing. And I was one of those listeners fascinated by this existentially interesting situation: the speaker who denies his function and puts the listeners into a questionable role too: how can we be an audience if the speaker doesn't have anything to say to us?

The audience needs to feel that the material is important. If as an audience member I feel that the subject *matters* to you as the presenter – better, that you are *passionate* about it, then I will be attracted to what you have to say. When presenters (on radio) say – 'Don't touch that dial!' or, (on TV or radio coming up to the commercial break) – 'Don't go away!' – they try to persuade the audience to stick with them because there is something important coming up that concerns them, that will be of interest to them, that they will not want to miss: something that connects the audience to the material. The material matters.

Like the audience, the material and your relationship to it merits a chapter to itself in this book. If there is one slogan that I use over and over again to persuade trainee broadcasters to focus it is:

'It's not how you say it, it's what you say.'

COMMUNICATION

It seems a given that what is going on must include communication, since if we are not communicating then we might as well pack up and go home. There are times however when we are involved in writing or ad-libbing on air, or trying to put our point across to our perceived audience and what we need to ask ourselves is precisely: are we communicating? I sometimes think that it would be useful if we could, like a teacher, issue a test to our audience afterwards about what we had been talking about. How confident are we that they would show good comprehension of what we had been on about?

Radio listeners tend to listen individually but often while doing something else (driving, eating, getting up in the morning); whereas television viewers typically watch in twos or threes and are more attentive but not exclusively so. They often talk and look away.

Neither audience is one hundred per cent attentive. Nor does communication happen because of the simple imparting of information. The intonation of what is said is often as important as the words used. An audience also picks up what is being presented to them through pictures (on TV) and by sometimes only partly listening to a radio broadcast. The audience's attention may be compromised by voluntary action – concentration being distracted, leaving the room; or by involuntary action – when there are competing sounds or interruptions.

As on-air performers therefore we must expect our audience to be only partly attentive and take corresponding measures. In thinking about our audience it may be as well to have their lack of attention in mind. But we must try to help the process of communication along by asking ourselves how easy is it for our audience to understand what we are saying. We must be concise, clear, simple and underline the essentials of what we are trying to get over to our audience. This can be achieved by the simple techniques discussed in this book.

TALENT OR KNOW-HOW?

Some people feel that they cannot read a script, or will never be able to perform well in front of people or a camera or microphone. I believe that anyone can learn simple techniques to get text 'off the page', and get information 'over' on mic or camera. It is true that the camera seems to like certain people more than others, that some first-timers even relax on camera and for them it seems easy to communicate. However what an audience always recognises is that someone has something interesting and informed to say. The right of the person to be in front of the camera or microphone is established not because they are merely relaxed or looking good, but because they are engaging us with what they are saying. That takes preparation, expertise, know-how. And it is that which we can focus on here.

Most of us are very critical when we hear or watch ourselves on playback. That is a natural response. Remember that it is a recording – and all recordings distort. You are also probably focussing on aspects that others ignore. 'Does my nose look that big?' 'I sound so artificial' etc. Think instead about your concentration. Were you thinking about what you were talking about? Even if you are very pleased with what you see, I would say the same to you. When watching playback be critical but constructive and think about what you are trying to get across.

SELF-AWARENESS, SELF-CONSCIOUSNESS, SELF-OBSESSION

It's all about me! Or is it? Let's deal with these three in turn.

Self-awareness

It is always good to be aware of how you are coming across. If you have your hair in your eyes, or what you say is confusing because of a fluff or a slip of the tongue then that will mar your performance and your audience will not focus on what you are telling them as they should. It can be corrected immediately. In an outside broadcast if your message is drowned by a passing aeroplane or pneumatic drill then it will not come across. A producer or technician would normally alert you to such things. As you watch playback you should be positively critical of things which were in your power to change to improve your performance. Being aware of these things at the time of recording or broadcast would have been best but will come with experience.

Self-consciousness

Self-consciousness is not so helpful and is often the reason for feeling nervous on air. People feel self-conscious when they have to present something they are not happy about. It is also a common anxiety dream. Being in front of people, the camera, the mic without a script and without anything to say and the audience watches and waits and you are feeling you want to be swallowed up – to somehow disappear. But even when you do have something to say, your nerves may get the better of you. Some people find it very difficult to shift their consciousness away from themselves and fear they will always be nervous of presentation. There are, however, two other elements of presentation which are more important than yourself which require your attention more than you do. They are your material and your audience. Once you manage to shift your attention to them you are on your way to dealing with nerves and self-consciousness. There will be more on nerves in Chapter 3.

Self-obsession

Self-obsession happens perhaps only in the eye of the beholder. It is only a problem if your audience senses it. I am not judging personal behaviour or psychology here: whether or not you are self-obsessed is not a matter for me, but if I can perceive it as a member of your audience then it might be a problem, but only in so far as it impedes your presentation. It may do that for instance in a situation where you are interviewing someone and the audience gets the feeling that you think you or your ideas are more important than your interviewee and what they have to say; or where the audience is being constantly reminded that it is you who is presenting your material, and so they are being asked to focus on you rather than what you are telling them. That is not to say that if you are dee-jaying a pacey music show with lots of gossip and personality you shouldn't be personable and someone with whom your young audience can identify. They will want you to be articulate, gobby, gossipy, have streetwise slang at your finger tips and perhaps be flirty with them and your guests. That may open you to the charge of self-obsession, but I would welcome that in the context of getting your material over to your audience.

YOUR OWN 15 MINUTES OF FAME

We live, we are told, in the UK at least, in a world obsessed by celebrity. Some wish to acquire celebrity status through appearing on the media as presenters or their guests. And yet perhaps because of the popularity of reality TV shows, it seems that those who enjoy such status acquired it with no effort. Even footballers and musicians have to remind us that they worked hard to rise to the top of their trees. I say *even* since actors are sometimes mocked as 'luvvies' for referring to their craft as work when some would perceive their celebrity as an anointment rather than as a consequence of having been in – *worked* in – a lot of films. Likewise some presenters are thought to belong to this exclusive club, but they did not get there without effort and those interested in presentation who think that it offers an easy pass to this club will be disappointed.

As a journalist, interviewer or programme host you may be rubbing shoulders with celebs. Indeed your contact book may be important in helping you to get work, although probably more as producer than presenter. Getting tables in restaurants can be useful, and being recognised in the street is fun. But celebrity is fickle and even if it lasts longer than 15 minutes, Andy Warhol coined the phrase to remind us that it always has a finite time span. Whether you become a celebrity is not an issue in the acquisition of presentation skills, but presentation skills alone do not provide access to it.

Preparation and Study

Generally, being prepared will be rewarded by a more polished performance even when the material is seemingly ad-libbed. Music presenters, who link the music with amusing anecdotes or information about the bands they are playing, often sound as if they are making it up as they go along, even when there is a lot of information in their links. That should give you a clue that they are not doing that, that what they say has been well prepared – in some cases even scripted. Radio music stations are very disciplined about what they play and require the presenters to be equally disciplined about what they say. In any case the best ad-libs are those that have been well prepared.

Likewise in television most presentation involves either a script or detailed agreement between presenter and producer/director. There is not a lot of room for manoeuvre. And yet the audience still has the impression that the presenter is making it up as they go along. It is almost a constituent of good presentation. That is not to say there is not room for off-the-cuff remarks or supplementary material that the presenter judges to be relevant during the broadcast. But even those parts will be based on adequate preparation and research.

Live news programmes offer occasional opportunity to think on your feet, especially when things go wrong. But, again, 'being across' the news will be your lifeline if the autocue stops, or a line goes down, or there is one of any number of possible technical hitches in the gallery. You will appreciate this even more in a situation where you are not prepared. And however well you get out of a hole it will be evident that thorough preparation is always prudent.

The Media Today

The media are not confined to radio and television, and those two media are now almost unrecognisable from what they were 20 years ago. Think of the TV channels available now and what they offer. Flick the dial on the radio and take note of the variety of listeners catered for. Outside those two the obvious area of expansion and innovation is the Internet, which changes and develops so quickly that to write about it invites the possibility of obsolescence between report and publication. That said the Internet is also a publisher of material produced and intended for radio and TV. Even presentation direct to Internet will often be derivative of techniques used on radio and TV. Two important aspects of the Internet come to mind. Its interactivity requires that you engage with your audience – much as you would do in a live interview or phone-in programme. And your writing skills will be required where you are also providing material on line.

Webcasts and podcasts are also new forms of publishing presentation material, but in essence do not differ a great deal from TV and radio as far as technique goes. However those that do them are often not experienced practitioners in radio and TV and so this book is also for them. Much of what applies to radio and TV will apply to web and podcasting. Bear in mind that with the web the reception may well be inferior to normal TV reception, and podcasts are necessarily up to date but recorded, and need to reflect immediacy without actually being live.

There are of course also many other forms requiring presentation skills: voice-overs, commercials, documentary films, corporate videos, shopping channels; hospital, shopping and community radio. The skills I address myself to in this book can be applied to all these and others.

SUMMARY

1. Presentation usually involves formality, the public and a transfer of information.
2. Other professionals use presentation skills but still find media presentation a challenge because of its different function.
3. Presence and thinking on your feet are useful, but focus of attention is essential. Presenter, audience and material compete for this focus.
4. Communication happens in a variety of ways, as does the behaviour of the audience.
5. Talent helps but material is important. Be only a constructive self-critic.
6. Be aware of how you are coming across. Do not be overcome by self-consciousness – the audience and the material are more important. And self-obsession is OK as long as the audience does not get the feeling that you think you are more important than the material. You may become a celeb, but for how long?
7. It may sound ad-libbed, but it is well prepared. Do your homework.
8. Web and podcasting offer new challenges although the skills necessary are similar to those for TV and radio.

Qualities of good presentation 2

Is good presentation science or art?

An honest answer to such a question has to acknowledge that although presentation is not an exact science, it does have qualities which can be defined. Is it art though? It may occasion a personal reaction in the audience similar to that of other artistic endeavours. And it is useful to remember that an audience's judgement can be personal, certainly individual, and sometimes even incomprehensible. Viewers and listeners are quick to tell you what they like and more often what they do not like, and even more *who* they like and do not like. The presenter may remind the viewer of their son, or who they would like for a daughter-in-law.

This is hardly helpful to the person in front of the camera or microphone. And finding something that works – the right formula – can seem to happen by chance. Some presenters find an original style which clicks with the audience. They may have tried various things, but it is likely that they did not try them out scientifically or methodically. They may just have happened on something.

Rules to be broken

Can we however decide on some qualities which a would-be performer in front of the mic or camera needs to think about – some ground rules?

We are going to try, bearing in mind that rules are there to be broken. If I say, as I do, that a presenter should be natural and articulate, then would I have to say a successful presenter who very much acted a character was an anomaly? And the same for a voice-over artist who spoke with a very strong regional accent which was hard to understand. I can, without effort, think of examples of both who are currently working successfully. Nevertheless I suggest that before you break the rules you need to understand them, and then find your niche. These qualities will help you find your voice and on-camera persona. They are foundations. Beyond them will be your individual contribution.

What is needed therefore is a list of qualities that will be useful to slot in to the back of your mind, to be kept there for you to access as a professional media performer. What will be occupying the front of your mind will be your material and the myriad of technical and practical matters which normally compete for your attention in a radio or TV environment.

THE FOUR GROUPS OF QUALITIES

The audience may judge you personally but if they were given a questionnaire to fill in on your performance they might come up with a more useful response if the questions were based on these qualities. You might like to check yourself against these qualities as you watch playback of your performance or that of others – and most apply to both audio and video.

I have divided the qualities into four groups to distinguish their function and how we think of them. This will help you to focus on, and apply them.

1. Communicative qualities
2. Material qualities
3. Personal qualities
4. Vocal qualities

1. Communicative qualities

The communicative qualities are clarity, articulacy, focus, confidence, energy, authority, adaptability to audience and station style.

Clarity

Your audience needs to understand you. You might for instance have a strong regional or non-native accent, which is fine, but if your audience cannot tell what you are saying, then you will lose their attention and they may switch off. And not only your speech must be clear but also what you are telling them. Is it logical? Is it also appropriate for your perceived audience? When you have your audience in front of you, you can see whether what you are telling them is being understood. Since you are remote but nevertheless in their living rooms, kitchens or cars it is *as if* you have eye contact. You need to be sensitive to your audience's need to understand you. What if, for instance, English is not the native language of some of your audience? You will have to take that into account, if you are an international broadcaster, and make sure you are clear enough for their comprehension.

If you mumble or fluff (stumble over a word) ask yourself whether the audience has understood what you said. If not, repeat it. When you listen back ask others if what you are saying can easily be understood.

Articulacy

You must not only be clear but also articulate. If you make the grammatical errors that may be made everywhere around you, then you are making a very strong statement about who you are and are inviting the audience to judge you. 'We wasn't there', 'I aren't going' barely raise an eyebrow on the bus, but mark an on-air performer. Even if you are trying to identify with an audience that would use such grammar you need to get your information over in the simplest way, and lazy grammar which is used on the street between people who know each other is inappropriate on air. Exceptions to this would include playing a character or acting a character in a story, but you would need to ask yourself always what gets the information over in the simplest and clearest way.

Remember you are not on the street or at home having a conversation with your friends or family where communication often goes into a kind of short form because of the familiarity.

It is all right in those environments to be semi-articulate because what you say is intended for those ears and eyes only and communication can happen without further effort. It may also be appropriate in a familiar environment to use words which on the air would make an exaggerated statement – such as swear-words or dialect. Acknowledge the different environments and ask yourself what is appropriate.

Focus

Usually there are restrictions of time to any broadcast and whatever your part is – whether interviewer, interviewee, presenter or guest – you will be asked to respect the clock. You will therefore need to be focussed on what you want to get across. Being focussed will also help if you have no script or you are trying to do a piece to camera without autocue. In those situations you need to keep in mind key words or facts, bullet points if you like, which will help you get your points across. It will help to prevent rambling or waffling. You will be using words off the top of your head but you will be on a mission to serve the information. Watching others perform or watching oneself on playback, it is easy to identify the moments when there is a lack of focus. It involves concentration. And staying focussed is especially necessary when there are so many distractions around you, as is the case in TV studios particularly. Location broadcasting outside the studio can attract a lot of attention. Focus will sometimes be your salvation from distraction and the resulting lack of concentration.

Confidence

Most qualities are inter-related: concentration and focus, credibility, intelligence and authority, for example. None more so than confidence which comes with so many other qualities in tow. Confidence also comes with experience. It is difficult to be confident if it is your first time on air, or if experienced, first time at a new station or network. Lack of confidence may come from self-consciousness. In that case you need to focus and concentrate on your material. It may come from lack of preparation or unfamiliarity with the material. Do your homework. Because performing on air gets better the more you do it confidence is built through experience. You get to take charge – to inhabit the space in front of the mic or camera. You come to belong there. It becomes your show even if it isn't. When you are speaking it should be. And although there is the danger of over-confidence when things can go wrong, experience should alert you to that fault too.

In live broadcasting when something goes wrong, as it inevitably will eventually, then the confident performer may even enjoy the opportunity to remind the audience that it is live, and that technical hitches do sometimes happen. In such a situation you can even learn to relax as you share the problem with the audience until it is fixed or you decide to move on to the next item, whatever is most convenient. Only a confident performer can achieve that, and needs to.

Energy

Presentation is a dynamic activity. It is fuelled by adrenaline, and requires energy. In some programming this is evident through style – for example where the audience is young. Music or comedy shows often boast lots of energy to keep the excitement up and the laughter going. But there cannot be a successful show where the red light heralding the start of transmission or recording doesn't bring a surge of energy through the veins of the performer. Energy is life. This is a natural human quality. Where it is lacking then often so are other essentials: creativity, interest and enthusiasm. Energy is an attractive quality and it joins the performer to the audience.

At a radio station I was working for I was once told by a studio technician that the presenter of a show he was working on fell asleep during a late-night current affairs programme. Presumably he was preceded into the land of nod by most of his audience, since if it was that boring or he was that tired, nothing much of interest was being broadcast.

Authority

Authority is the natural consequence of good material. You cannot impose it or bolt it on. The audience will believe what you say and respect you if you show that what you say is in good faith. If you are relating something contentious or opinionated for example in politics or criticism, they may not agree with you but they will recognise your right to say it and the fact that your opinion is researched and prepared.

Authority also comes from the radio or TV station you are working for. The BBC is known throughout the world for its impartiality and this is one of the reasons its news service is so popular. The BBC brand gives authority to the presenters it employs. Some however think that the BBC represents Britain's colonial past – its authority perceived as authoritarian. Voice of America is known for its close relationship with the US State Department – what it broadcasts will be judged accordingly.

Authority is therefore a subject for discussion and trust. When government meddles in media matters then the media's authority is called into question. Journalistic authority therefore comes from resisting political pressure. This is easier in some parts of the world than others.

Adaptability to audience and station style

Few on-air performers stick with one station, nor therefore with one audience. Different stations and networks go after a different share of the listening and viewing public. They do this through their programming schedule and in effect through choice of presenter and whom they have in front of the mic and camera. You need to know whom you are talking to, in order to successfully engage the audience. And as you become sensitive to performing to differing viewers and listeners you will become adept at adapting to them.

2. Material qualities

The material qualities are understanding, intelligence, interest, credibility and balance, accessibility, relevance and topicality.

Understanding

You are on the radio or TV for a reason. Are you entertaining, informing or educating? You have a job to do. And to do it you have prepared. You may look, like many successful performers, as if you are making it up as you go along, but if you are (making it up as you go along), you may well fall flat on your face. And the success of your mission on the media may well be judged on *what* you are telling your audience, as well as how you are telling it.

The reason why journalists generally make better newsreaders and presenters than actors, is that they bring to a news cast their experience and knowledge of current affairs. They read with understanding. An actor may have a 'beautiful voice' (whatever that is), but you immediately notice, unless they are also well informed in current affairs, that their reading lacks context. It is not just what is on the page, it is also the subtext and what has gone before that inform good news presentation. There will be more on this in Chapter 5.

Intelligence

Intelligence in this context is nothing to do with IQ. It is not about how many books you have read or qualifications you have. It is about engaging your brain in the presentation process. It is knowing what the options are if something is not going to plan. It is being prepared. It is bringing particular expertise to bear to make your mark and put your stamp on the programme. It is popping in an unexpected question in an interview because it is appropriate. It is thinking ahead. It is knowing what to do when the lines go down or the printer jams and you have no script on a live broadcast. One broadcaster I trained at the BBC told me how he spoke live for 15 minutes without a script on a current affairs radio programme, because of printer and computer problems. He could do this because he knew what he was talking about.

Interest

The content of what you are saying, the 'what' of your presentation, must engage your audience. They may know nothing of the subject you are talking about, but you must be convinced that you can command their interest. That what you are telling them is interesting. This may involve your passion for your subject. The producer, editor, station or network manager may all have ideas about what is of interest to the audience they are trying to attract, but as presenter or studio guest, you must assume it as you present, because it is part of the process. And you can attract your audience to your subject matter quite simply through your interest in it.

Credibility and balance

A TV or radio performer will earn trust if the truth of what they are saying is confirmed, even if it takes time. But then credibility is often earned by the station or network rather than the individual presenter, and over a period of time. I have heard the phrase 'not wrong for long' used to describe a 24-hour news network which, in its effort to be first on the air with a news story, was sometimes sloppy about checking the facts before broadcasting. If you are on the air to provide information and if it can easily be established that what you are saying is wrong, or you have to change the story, then you will lose credibility.

And then there is opinion. Variety is of interest to an audience. They want to hear the debate. It should be a balanced debate. If you give one strongly held view point you should balance it with another opposing one. Some presenters and stations peddle extreme points of view. 'Shock jocks' are there to provoke. Radio phone-in presenters like to get things going with provocative points of view. But the audience quickly realises what is happening and on some programmes do not expect a balanced current affairs debate. You do not need to assume the audience will agree with you, but to be credible you must be sincere. Your audience will trust you if what you have to say is useful and honest.

Accessibility

As a material quality accessibility means making what you have to say easy to grasp for your perceived audience. As with credibility this is a journalistic quality. If you were writing your presentation for a newspaper what would the sub-editors do with your copy to make it easy on the readers? How can you therefore make it easier for your viewer/listener to grasp what you have to tell them? You will need to think about the language you use to connect your subject to your audience.

People who need to work on accessibility on the media include academics, experts, writers, musicians, and creative people. If you are interviewing them then you need to bridge the gap between their 'expertise' and the audience's understanding by asking them to explain or elucidate so the audience can access their knowledge. If you are one of these people, then honestly ask yourself: how accessible is my expertise?

Relevance and topicality

You must keep up with your audience. If they feel what you are saying is in any way out of date or irrelevant, then you will lose them. You need to be an authority on your subject and failure to make that plain will dilute your presence. As you focus on your material then that becomes all-important. If you are in news or current affairs then the story changes quickly and you need to be across it. With feature material and music you need to be informed and understand that the audience wants to keep up with what is going on out there. You are the conduit. Earn their respect with information and research. Keep up.

3. Personal qualities

The personal qualities are being natural, personality, engagement, passion and enthusiasm, warmth and friendliness, concentration.

Being natural

It is tricky being yourself, professionally. I know it seems odd – who else can you be? But it can take time to find your on-air personality. It is something which is part of the medium itself and operates in relation to it. It is not existential, it is functional, which means that it is to do with why you are on the air. Actors seem to have a problem with it, since they ask 'Who do you want me to be?' They expect and can *deliver* 'a newsreader', or 'a mumsy daytime features presenter'. It is true some actors move into presentation successfully but they need to get over this early hurdle and learn to be themselves on camera or mic. It is immediately noticeable and unsatisfactory if they *play* a newsreader, instead of just reading the news (not that it is easy).

What you say on air needs to flow through you and your on-air persona is there to allow it to happen. You are the conduit.

Personality

So how do you find this on-air personality? The simple answer is through the audience. You are having a relationship with the audience and in their company you will find your identity. For beginners it may take some time as you establish this relationship, but it should be a natural consequence of talking to your audience. When you have a conversation with a person for the first time they get an impression of your personality. They may not yet have an opinion, but one is doubtless forming. It is a human reaction. And it is what goes on between the presenter and presented-to, and allows you to communicate with your audience. You stop reading to them or performing for the camera and start talking to them directly.

Then, I am afraid, they start to judge you. They start to like or dislike you. They will react to you, and it may seem alarming. There is not a lot you can do, as you are in their living rooms and cars, and they can decide to turn you off for no better reason than you remind them of their mother or they don't like your nose or your jokes or what you are telling them. Hopefully others will have a more favourable reaction.

Engagement

You know how many it takes to tango. Well, it takes no fewer to present: the presenter and the presented-to. And, although some forget, the more important of the two is the presented-to. Of course hopefully there will be more than one but, however many there are, your business is to engage them, and to be sensitive to when you do that successfully or not. Your awareness of your audience will have an effect on how your presentation goes. If the programme is in any way interactive then engagement is easier. For instance the phone-in radio programme or any TV programme with a live studio audience demands that you engage with the phone-in guest or live audience, and so will help you engage with the wider audience 'out there'. With recorded programmes, or a news cast, relating to the audience can be more difficult but no less essential.

Passion and enthusiasm

Whatever the subject matter of a programme, if the presenter or interviewee is passionate about their subject then the audience will be interested. Perhaps not for long, but they will be initially engaged. And in today's media world of channel and bandwidth choice you will be encouraged to hook your audience with your passion. It is your passion that people relate to *before* your material, and although it is not the only quality you need, it is an essential one. It is true of course that an academic can be passionate about his or her subject but their style of delivery may only attract a small informed or learning audience. But someone who doesn't care about their material – and you hear some newsreaders being bored by their stories (perhaps because they have been reading the same news all day) – will always be a turn off.

Warmth and friendliness

What is the relationship you have with your audience? Is it formal? Is it intimate? It is surely somewhere in the middle. It is hopefully warm and friendly partly because that will help you establish a relationship with them, and that, in turn, will help you get your material across in the most efficacious way. The relationship is perhaps that of an acquaintance.

It may sometimes be helpful to think of selling: as customers we have all had the experience of salespeople who do not seem to care whether we buy from them or not; whereas in those shops where they greet with a smile, are generally helpful and willing to chat, even if their hope for a sale fuels this courtesy, we will surely be more encouraged to buy. Likewise the audience will be more receptive and inclined to stay with you if the relationship is warm and inviting.

Another reason you need to be on good and friendly terms with your audience is that you are after all being invited to enter their cars, living rooms, kitchens, even bedrooms, and it is as well to respect that invitation.

Concentration

Concentration is an important quality that you yourself are in the best position to recognise. If you are focussed on what you are talking about – not distracted by the many things that go on in radio, and even more, TV studios – then you will succeed in getting across not only what you have to say but also yourself. If you lose it then you will certainly notice it on the playback, but hopefully others will not if you are able to cover up your distraction. Your concentration is your salvation in difficult situations: with a difficult interviewee, for example, or a delicate question if you are the interviewee, a technical fault in a live broadcast, or a fluff. If you keep with your material and focus, your concentration will reward you.

4. Vocal qualities

The vocal qualities are variety, intonation, correct emphasis, colour, pace, relaxation.

Variety

Many people find they have monotonous voices when they hear themselves on playback. It is more of a problem on radio where your voice has more to do to paint the pictures and tell the story. In order to find a larger range there are useful exercises which you will find in Chapter 3 of this book. It is a good idea to think about your voice as a musical instrument on which for instance you can play a scale. If you have ever read a story to a child, think about how you animated it to engage the child's interest. If you read it flat, then you probably lost your young audience. You probably had to exaggerate your intonation to increase the interest of the story. The same technique is used in lifting a script off the page. You need to explore the possibilities your voice can provide.

Intonation, correct emphasis, colour

Intonation is the music of the voice. In conversation we quite naturally employ various vocal techniques to convey meaning. Intonation is as important as the words themselves in the business of communication. The problem is that as soon as we become conscious of such variations we are prone to sound artificial. This becomes evident when reading scripts. Good intonation is informed by the comprehension of what you are saying and sounds natural because you go up and down and emphasise for a reason, which is not pre-decided. Presenting needs to do the same.

Correct emphasis, which is effortless in conversation since it is informed by our mission to communicate something, becomes a chore in reading a script. We need to decide which words or phrases to emphasise to get the meaning across.

Colour then makes the text interesting. Railway station announcements lack colour, even when they are not automated. Voice-overs on commercials are full of it to get you to buy the product. Presenters need to decide how much to give to their radio scripts or pieces to camera to engage their audience. Inexperienced presenters often know they lack the vocal flexibility to add colour (sounding monotonous), but are not sure how to find more flexibility. There are some useful techniques to learn to add colour.

Pace

Pace, which includes rhythm, is not quite the same as speed which is about words per second. Pace varies and can be used effectively to tell the story. Notice how people naturally pace their conversation. We all have a natural pace: some people speak quickly all the time, others – and they are rarer – speak in a very measured way. You need to be able to manage pace. We vary pace for effect, and need to do it presenting a script. But as with most techniques it must be used with subtlety or the effect will be dissipated. Being nervous can speed you up. You may want to get to the end. But think of your audience – if you go too fast you will lose them.

Talking to time is very important in broadcasting, both in TV and radio. You may have to alter your pace to take on the demands of the clock, but you must make sure that what you say remains clear and comprehensible. There will be more on this in Chapters 6 and 7.

Relaxation

All performing – from opera singing to triple-jumping – benefits from relaxation. It calms the mind and allows the performer to excel. Its effects are chiefly psychological, and are all the more powerful for being so. Most performers feel nervous prior to the gig and are right to be concerned if the butterflies are absent. You need to get the butterflies to fly in formation: to get the energy produced by the nerves to work for you. And however you relax, be it by breathing, doing yoga, even lying flat on your back, the benefits are self-evident, and contrast well to those times when you allowed stress and tension for whatever reason, (and there are plenty in media presentation) to influence your offer. A relaxed presenter can think on their feet and bring that little something extra which makes the provision to relax worthwhile.

SUMMARY

1. The personal side of presentation cannot be quantified or even defined. But we can agree on certain objective qualities.
2. There are four types of qualities: communicative, material, personal and voice qualities.
3. Communicative qualities allow you to be clear and focussed and make it easy for the audience to understand what you are telling them.
4. Material qualities allow you to relate what you have to say to your audience – make it relevant and accessible to them.
5. How are you coming across? What is your relationship with your audience? Personal qualities include warmth and friendliness but also enthusiasm for your subject.
6. How can you perfect your vocal instrument to make it do what you want? Give your presentation colour, interest and pace. Vocal qualities will help the expression of your ideas.

Voice and breathing 3

WHY DO BROADCASTERS NEED VOICE TRAINING?

It would be hard to overestimate the value of proper attention to voice and breathing in presentation. Voice and breathing exercises can be as useful to someone speaking on radio and TV as they are to an opera singer. Some of the same techniques used by professional singers and actors can be used to facilitate effective presentation. Having said that they are unfortunately not often part of a presenter's routine preparation. And scant, although increasing, attention is paid to voice training in broadcast journalism courses. If you have ever run out of breath while delivering a script or speech you will know that the physicality of voice and breathing can fail you at important moments.

It is of course equally true and important to note that in normal conversation we hardly ever think about intonation, pitch, breathing or suchlike. They just come naturally, or do they? Well, they should do in normal conversation. How can they look after themselves in 'normal' conversation when they can be such an issue in presenting? Why do presenters complain of running out of breath or getting the intonation or emphasis wrong? If you make demands on your voice through any kind of professional speaking – and here I include teaching, reading, speechmaking, addressing small teams as well as broadcasting, anything in fact which requires you to communicate to a group – then you need to think about voice and breathing techniques.

With radio and TV presentation we use our voices in a conversational way. Unlike singers and theatre actors, for instance, we do not normally need to project. Indeed it is part of the technique of effective presentation that we seem to be having a conversation with our audience (as I point out elsewhere in this book). But in order to do that effectively, especially if there is a script involved, we will need voice technique.

INTONATION AND VOCAL VARIETY

A catch-all word, intonation refers to the music of speech. Voices that lack it sound monotonous. Too much variety of tone can produce a sing-song effect which is equally counterproductive. There are elements of intonation which are worth detailing since they can be looked at separately according to what may need attention. These elements are used by us (sometimes unconsciously in conversation) to deliver meaning and emphasis.

Pitch

The level on the scale that your voice can go through is effectively used to add meaning. When you listen to yourself on playback note the variations of pitch. Variation of pitch denoting new sentences, and therefore new thoughts and ideas keep the listener engaged. Headlines in a news bulletin should start on different notes to vary the delivery and maintain interest in each new story. Sentences can be ended on a downward inflection or an upward one with different effect.

But first you must discover your own range and ability to use it.

EXERCISE

Try going up and down your scale to find your range:

phrase,

a *and*

with *then*

scale *try*

the *coming*

up *down*

going *with*

Try *another*

You do not need to use my words. Take any sentence and play around with the pitch. But try to make it sound natural. It may feel artificial at first, but you need to find a way of building in differing pitch which will enhance the meaning.

It is usual to go down at the end of a sentence but you can choose to go up. A higher pitch is sometimes used to create emphasis. We use variations of pitch to aid meaning. We go up on certain words to lift them out of the monotony of the phrase. If you listen to a recording of your voice (or someone else's) notice how you pick out certain words for emphasis and how you might do that by going up on certain words.

Going up at the end of a phrase or sentence keeps the idea open, and also keeps the audience interested; although it can indicate a question and uncertainty. You can also come down on words at the end of a phrase to give a feeling of finality and closure. The downward inflection concludes and finishes. The upward inflection invites interest in what comes after.

Beware, however, of sounding artificial. While it is often good to end phrases on an upward inflection, in English we use a more complicated music to indicate the subtlety of what we say, so you should avoid simplistic inflection decisions. Allow the sense of what you are saying to dictate the inflections, as you do in normal conversation.

Female voices

Some women in broadcasting complain that their voices seem too high pitched and consequently, they often think, lack authority. They think they sound girly. It is true of course that women have higher voices than men. And some have famously, with a questionable degree of success, tried to change them. Margaret Thatcher comes to mind. You have to be careful. Often people judge themselves harshly when listening to recordings. Women sometimes think they sound too young for an audience to take them seriously. But remember your own judgement may not be shared by the majority of your audience.

Even if your pitch is high and that is natural to you, people will get used to you and soon focus on what you are telling them rather than on the pitch of your voice. Our voices are like our faces – they are unique. They come in all shapes and sizes. The authority comes from what you are telling the audience, not the pitch of your voice. I have heard war correspondents whose voices make them sound too young or immature to be in a war zone; yet they maintain their authority and the respect of their audience by the sheer weight and importance of what they are telling them.

There is however a natural way to lower your pitch. It involves resonance. There are resonators in the head, the mouth and the nose and also in the chest and even further down. The whole body can be used to resonate the sound made by our voices. To lower the voice pitch naturally one technique that can be used is to resonate the voice in the chest as well as in the head.

EXERCISE

Place a hand on your chest. Now start humming softly feeling the resonation in your head at first and then bring the sound down into the chest. Feel the vibration in your chest as you start to use the chest to resonate the sound. This will often be accompanied by a lowering of the note but that will be a natural response to using your chest resonator. Now try using sounds – the ones I use for articulation exercises (p.42) work here:

Moo Moh Maw Mar May Mee My Mow (as in 'now')

Now try using a sentence, any sentence.

You should recognise the difference of using resonance in the head, mouth, throat, etc. and that of the chest. Using the chest resonators gives the voice a more rounded and emotionally fuller force. You will be more committed to the content, and consequently so will your audience. People who habitually use head resonators lack this. Bringing it down you can experience a more centred, emotional, 'whole' sound from your voice. You may even find a range you did not even think you had.

Pace

Because pace involves rhythm it can include a variation in speed and the use of pause for effect. If for instance you pause before a word or phrase you give extra weight and interest to it. Likewise pausing after a phrase can lift its importance. Try it with a piece of text and see how you can effect a change of overall meaning. Watch out for over-use of pause – the effect will be diminished if used too much.

The pressure to speed up

There are many temptations to speed up, not least the ubiquity and importance of the clock and timing. There is a natural tendency to speed up if someone is warning you that you only have 15 seconds left or you can see the clock and need to be out by a certain time. We will deal with talking to time later, but there are other temptations to speed up (many more than those to slow down), and they should generally be resisted.

Speed is personal. Some people naturally speak quicker than others – some remain articulate and engaging – others speak quickly because they are nervous and unconfident in real life. You do not want to catch their habit. Speaking too quickly on radio and TV often indicates nervousness – sometimes simply a desire to get it over with! Speaking too quickly is often accompanied by fluffs and mistakes – they should be a warning to slow down.

How to slow down

The antidote to speaking too quickly is to think of your audience. Are they able to digest what you are telling them? If not you must slow down to accommodate them. If they cannot understand you then you are not communicating. Some people find slowing down more difficult than others, precisely because it is to do with confidence and personality. If you can see your audience (perhaps only one person) you will soon realise when they are and, more importantly, when they are not taking in what you are telling them. Try, for instance, reading to a child too quickly – a young audience will soon show you whether they are attending to what you are telling them.

Vocal variety

There are several ways to introduce vocal variety into your presentation. For instance news bulletin stories often contain antithesis: 'On the one hand the Israelis said this, on the other hand the Palestinians said that.' The inclination is to go up on 'this' and down on 'that' to indicate the two sides. But beware of the pitfalls of hackneyed rhythms and intonations which presenters have learned from each other which is why they are sometimes so successfully lampooned. Monty Python did it with the phrase '... and now for something completely different', which mimicked TV presentation of the time when the presenter moves artificially on to a new topic. Also there is the habit of always going down on the last two or three words (which among others Jeremy Clarkson is apt to do, for effect):

'Here is a visual example of that'.
doing just

'And now for something different'.
completely

Projection

Projection is a vocal technique associated more with the theatre than the TV or radio studio, where a performer needs to be heard at the back of the gallery without the aid of amplification, and yet not shout. It is about taking in your audience, and is useful for the presenter when distinguishing between intimate and declamatory and the range in between.

Think late-night jazz radio on the one hand and a youth programme such as 'Don't Forget your Toothbrush' on the other. Or even time of day – breakfast and dinner – 'wakey wakey' in the morning and the more intimate 'whisper' late at night.

Watch and listen

Watch how others use vocal variety, not only in the media but also in conversation. You will surely already be doing it yourself to aid expression and meaning. You need to become aware of what you may have taken for granted. This will be especially useful if you are not used to reading scripts and need to inject some life into them, as you will see in Chapter 6.

BREATHING

It's natural, isn't it?

Breathing, like presentation itself, is not something we are normally aware of until there is a problem. We must however devote time to understanding it in order to not only prevent future problems but also to be able to ignore it. Just as we do not focus on our breathing when speaking in a conversation nor do we want to be thinking about it when we are presenting. And yet it does come up when we run out of breath, sentences are too long or we are in some other way not in as much control of our speech as we would like to be, often when reading a script.

'It's as natural as breathing.' If this describes something which is as unconscious as it is artless, then it is surely useful to us in our pursuit of improved presentation. It is as well to point out here that breathing, as that essential life-giving activity, is of great interest to students of yoga and meditation. Focus on it can discipline and quieten the mind and aid physical posture. In the same way good breathing can aid good vocal expression, and mental acuity.

We need breath to express ourselves, but we also require something extra from our breathing mechanisms to fuel the increased demand as we speak professionally. And we want even that enhanced process to be natural, especially as we are often giving the impression that our presentation is like conversation.

Some exercises that give us more breath will help us with our increased requirement and yet those demands will not be evident. Basically we can gain more breath by breathing more deeply. But by deep I don't mean just taking in more volume of breath – although that is a consequence – but taking it in further down, filling not only the upper chest but also the belly, the centre of the body.

EXERCISE

Stand up with your feet about shoulder width apart and facing front. Put a hand on your stomach. Breathing normally, feel the movement in that part of the body as you inhale and exhale. Now taking deeper breaths you will feel the increased movement in your abdomen. Breathing in through your nose to a count of three, feel your centre expand and move out, then after a moment (a magic one where there is no activity at all), breathe out to a count of five noticing the contraction of the muscles at the centre. Repeat several times. All the time you need to keep your shoulders and upper chest completely relaxed.

This may be easier to do after you have done some relaxation exercises. But one consequence of doing this breathing exercise, which I would recommend before any broadcast or presentation, is that it calms you down without taking away your alertness. It is however primarily concerned with relaxing your upper chest and shoulders and allowing you to draw in more breath to the centre of the body so that you will have more breath at your disposal.

RELAXATION

A confident performance usually comes from a relaxed performer. Presenters can borrow here usefully from actors and singers. Tension – the opposite of relaxation – will mar that performance and sap necessary energy. When it goes well there is a feeling that there is less effort and more concentration; that, to use a tennis analogy, you hit the 'sweet spot' and the ball consequently goes just where you want it to; that the script reads itself and you are on top form without trying to be. How do you create that feeling? How, when you are not feeling on form, can you get it back? In a word: discipline.

The discipline

Relaxation is a discipline in a TV or radio studio because with the amount of activity and stress around you, you will need discipline to be relaxed. And you need to relax to perform. How do you do that?

The best way to relax is to lie down, flat on the ground, going through each part of the body as you feel it getting heavier: starting with your limbs and coming up through your body to your shoulders, neck and finally head and face. Although you can try this at home it may not be practical in your work place. Not to worry: there are more discrete ways of doing relaxation exercises standing or even sitting.

You need to understand where the common areas of tension usually are. The neck, the shoulders and the face. And these parts are often on camera. So do this first exercise standing, or sitting if you must.

EXERCISE

If standing, let yourself go from the waist so that you are doubled up and your top half is relaxed and hanging, with your feet and legs tensed to take the weight. You are already focussing on your top half. From this doubled-up U position bring yourself back to standing slowly from the bottom up, feeling as your spine comes back to vertical that you are putting one vertebra on top of the other as you unfurl. Lastly your shoulders come back into place followed by your neck and head.

If you are sitting down you can do the following exercises in your chair, sitting in it four square, with both feet on the ground as if attached to the floor, and with a straight back. Comfortable but not slouched.

Now focus on your head and create a feeling that it is independent of the rest of your body. Think of a ping-pong ball on top of a jet of water, or a puppet on strings. Let it loll forward and then back and then bring it back to a neutral position. You can do a head roll as you loll it forward and gently roll it round noticing the tensions in your neck as you go. Do this gently. You cannot get rid of those tensions but you can become aware of them which is useful. Do that twice: once each way.

Now the shoulders. Roll one first forward then back, then the other the same, then both together. You can then roll them round in a rotary movement first forwards then backwards. Then tense them right up – shrugging, then letting them go. Repeat. And feel that they are dropped further down having done this. You need the shoulders to be heavy. Shake your arms and hands to get a feeling of relaxation in the shoulders.

You can follow this last little sequence with a 'centre-ing' exercise. The value of this is to focus on that most important part of the body which we call the centre, around your navel. This is a powerhouse and is an area which is very important in good voice production. It is the area into which you take your breath and it gives you a solidity, a full body stability and therefore authority. Recognise this after doing the following:

EXERCISE

Stand with your feet facing forward, shoulder width apart. You should be relaxed not stiff but straight, as you were, having come up from the bent forward pose in the exercise above. Close your eyes and let your knees bend slightly allowing the legs to sag a little. Take your attention within and to that centre just below the navel. Breathe into that area, softly; you can deepen it a little beyond a normal breath. While you are breathing into this area you can visualise an objective – perhaps your programme or script or what you are going to have to do. Feel the energy and allow it travel through you and outwards. This is a relaxing exercise but it is also an empowering one. It helps you concentrate, unify mind and body, letting the tension go and focussing your attention. Try it.

POSTURE

Voice production involves the whole body, not just because breathing involves a good deal of it, but because it is a very human activity. The voice reveals attitude. If you are tired or tense or emotional it will tell in your voice. If you speak while sitting slouched, for instance, then that is what you will sound like. If you are stiffly standing to attention then you will probably sound like a soldier on parade. If you are curled up on a comfy sofa talking to a friend on the phone we'll probably get the softer, relaxed, approachable side of you.

A neutral position

In order therefore to be in the best possible posture to be free to express a variety of tone and meaning if necessary, but not to feel bound by certain attitudes, then a good neutral position is advantageous. Standing and being centred (see above for the centre-ing exercise) is a strong position to be able to deliver whatever you like. Sitting at a desk or on a sofa on daytime TV tells a certain story about the programme content which you will want to be part of. Radio presenters usually sit, although for voice production it would be better if they stood. Deejays often stand and it gives them energy. But with a lot of technical equipment to operate and with scripts and papers in front of you, sitting at a sound desk is more practical for most radio. Remember, if you sit, to keep your feet four square on the ground as if you are plugged into the earth from where energy is coming to you, so you do not want to break contact. Make sure your chair is comfortable and adjustable to your height so that it allows you to sit straight.

Finally do not wear anything constraining around your waist. I have even seen radio presenters loosen their trousers as they prepare to go on air. It keeps that important centre of the body free and relaxed – even if it embarrasses the guests!

DEALING WITH NERVES

A greater problem

A greater problem than having nerves is not having them. Going on air or into a studio to record a piece and feeling no apprehension does not bode well. It is the same for all performers. Nerves are energy and that is a useful commodity in performance. You can turn that energy to your advantage, and use it to lift your game. Get those butterflies to fly in formation. But if you don't have that slightly uneasy feeling be on your guard, and if you have the opportunity look for signs of lack of concentration on the playback. Some, however, are disabled by nerves and that is counter-productive.

Some methods

Remember nerves are normal. Most people about to perform suffer from them, and more importantly even seasoned and well-known performers have them. So you are not on your own.

It is comforting to know, if you are a sufferer from nerves, that there are some simple ways of dealing with them. One quite basic method involves tensing the muscles of your abdomen and buttocks. Hold, release and repeat. I would add a version of my breathing exercise. (I think it is good anyway for anyone about to broadcast whether live or recorded.) Even with only five seconds to spare you can breathe into your abdomen and centre. With a bit more time I would suggest following the relaxation exercise above, but in any case do some deeper breathing which will have the effect of calming you without taking away the energy.

Another fundamental way of dealing with nerves is to take your focus away from yourself and into your material. You should also think about whom you are talking to – your audience. This will give you ample to think about and usefully not about yourself. You can never become too familiar with what you are about to tell your audience. And thinking about or visualising your audience (or an imaginary audience member) will help you tell your story effectively.

Voice exercises and articulation

The demands of broadcasting

Talk Radio is busiest at breakfast time. That's when most people listen to the radio – when they are getting up, having breakfast and going to work. Working on radio shows that start at 6 am or earlier involves a very early start, hopefully preceded by early to bed. Nevertheless, when you open that fader (i.e. open the microphone channel to speak), sometimes your voice surprises you especially if you have not warmed it up. It may croak, it may wheeze, it may not even seem connected to your brain. At BBC World Service which broadcasts live around the world, a huge number of listeners in the Indian subcontinent turn on their radio at breakfast which is around 01.30–02.00 am in the UK, and that means the broadcasters must sound fresh and lively even if they are coming to the end of a ten-hour shift. How can you do that? I would always recommend a voice warm-up, whether or not you are broadcasting at unsocial hours, but especially if you are.

Warm-up exercises

There are many warm-up routines and I recommend two or three excellent books written by the best voice teachers in the field which have much to say about voice exercises. I would suggest that you find your own which suits you and your requirements from the books I list in the Bibliography. Here I will outline a routine which I have found useful.

EXERCISE

Practise the following sounds, using the lips and muscles around the mouth to accentuate the articulation:

Moo Moh Maw Mar May Mee My (as in 'eye') *Mow* (as in 'now'). Then change the consonant but keep the vowel:

Voo Voh Vaw Var Vay Vee Vy Vow
Boo Boh Baw Bar Bay Bee By...etc.

Start slowly but then increase the speed as you get more confident. This exercise gets your lips, tongue and mouth going.

Massage your face and jaw, making sounds as you go. Become aware of the jaw joint so that your lower jaw can relax and sag and imagine that your upper jaw can float off upwards. This is a visualisation, of course, but it is useful to help loosen the jaw and get rid of tension. Let the lower jaw hang open as if you were acting like an idiot. Make an 'aah' sound. Feel how tense your jaw actually is.

In English it is best, for articulation, to keep the voice at the front of the mouth. That way you will enunciate well and what you say will be clear. Those upper-class accents you sometimes hear come from the back of the mouth and are neither easy on the ear nor good for the voice that produces them. Try the following phrase doing what it says and slightly exaggerate the enunciation:

'I must keep my voice at the front of my mouth.'

PROBLEMS AND WHAT YOU CAN DO ABOUT THEM

There are some problems which are not problems, some that can be dealt with, some that need referral to a specialist (a medical or a speech therapist) and some which cannot be corrected. You need to distinguish first what kind of problem you have if you have one at all.

Too high pitch

Some complain that their voice is too high or lacks authority – and I have dealt with that earlier. Either that is not a problem or one that can be dealt with, whichever way you come to see it. Remember that when listening to playback or ROT (recording off transmission) most people at first are very self-critical and not always usefully so, as they tend to focus on aspects that others do not notice. Pitch can be one of those kinds of problems.

Noisy mouth

Hearing the intake of breath or having too much saliva in the mouth are other common complaints. The intake of breath is not a problem – you have to breathe – it is a human necessity. But being short of breath can be corrected by breathing exercises as above. Too much saliva is also natural generally but you can try taking an intake of breath through the mouth before speaking, which can reduce the amount of saliva in the mouth. If, on the contrary, you suffer from a dry mouth biting your tongue gently can produce saliva. It is also as well to have water to hand to sip.

Sibilance, lisping and a weak 'r'

Sibilance is when the 's' sound whistles. It is caused by allowing the sound to come through an incorrectly formed tongue in relation to the mouth through which the sound passes. It is sometimes exaggerated by certain microphones. Some of the problem can be reduced by angling the mic so that you speak across it rather than directly to it. However you will need to see a speech therapist to find out if you can eradicate sibilance. This applies also to a lisp and a weak 'r' (where it comes out sounding like a 'w'); and the advice may be that you cannot correct the fault.

But is it a fault? If you have any of these speech peculiarities (if that is what one can call them), you may wish to ask yourself that if you have lived with them this far is there a good reason why you should not accept them as others will, including your audience? Famously Jonathan Ross, like the late Roy Jenkins did, lives with a weak 'r', and thrives on it. Other well-known people display what some may call speech defects including a stammer and they have come to be accepted for them. You may turn them to your advantage by making them part of your broadcast persona – something which identifies you and makes you stand out from the rest.

ACCENTS AND DIALECTS

We all have an accent. Our speech patterns are formed through habit – part of which is interaction with the environment and people around us. Speech is such that it is necessarily social and therefore is formed by two or more people speaking to each other. You will notice how quickly children pick up accents from their peers, but also dialects, slang and even foreign languages. But is your accent acceptable? Your peers, editors and bosses may comment and you will feel sensitive to their feedback. But what of the audience? They are the important ones. Perhaps they like your accent even if your colleagues tease you for it.

Is it clear?

I always ask myself when I hear someone with a strong accent: is what they are saying clear? Am I getting it? And again it is the question you should be asking of yourself: am I taking the audience with me? The odds are that relaxing into your own accent will give you confidence and make you feel more at home in front of the camera or mic. You will feel more yourself and that has got to be a good thing.

Suitability

However there is some debate as to whether a strong South London accent would be suitable for the news or a RP (received pronunciation) voice is suitable for a pop show? And there are cultural questions being raised here. It is not what people expect and that may work against you. Whether you think that is unfair or not is another matter. You can of course modify your accent to suit your material or your boss, but beware of sounding bizarre. Over-compensation towards the perceived acceptability of an accent can produce unnatural results, worse than the original. Happily it is becoming less necessary to doctor an accent, but audiences do have strong views on accents and so it is a contentious subject.

Cultural climate

In today's cultural climate in Britain, regional accents are much more acceptable than they were. It used to be the case that the BBC would only employ male English announcers with an accent from the South-East of the country. And if you listen to broadcasts from the 1950s and before that is what you got. Broadcasting is in a different age now and what you see on the screen or hear on the radio reflects the audience that is watching or listening to it. British society has changed a lot since the 1950s and so there's plenty of diversity to be seen and heard.

As attitudes change so do voices on the media. Class and education are less defined by accent nowadays. There may be an ongoing discussion about the media 'dumbing down' but as there are many more outlets now so there should be more room for all comers.

However, dialects and slang should be used with caution. Ask yourself if they include or exclude the audience: if the latter, they are counter-productive. Rappers and hip-hop deejays may use language which excludes many, but that may be the desired effect. Be careful not to be offensive. Swearing and using racist language are not only indefensible but will attract recrimination and may harm your broadcasting future. Having said that, the odd involuntary curse will sometimes indicate that you are human after all.

Non-native English speakers

If the English language belongs to those cultures or countries where speakers of English are most populous, then Britain would come well down the list. The Indian subcontinent would come top and so they could be said to have more claim on the language's development than users from other parts of the world. In Britain, with its large ethnic South Asian community, it would be odd if we did not hear a distinctive accent reflecting that. But there are also West Indian, West African, South African, Greek, Turkish and other Eastern European accents heard aplenty in Britain, reflecting recent immigration to the country from these areas of the world. I see no problem with accented English in the media, subject to the rules and qualities I have outlined elsewhere. Accents reflect society and so does the media.

American English

There could be more of a problem with American in Britain. An American accent indicates for some an American media product, which may be counter-productive. Some would say that there are too many American imports in the British media, and with their huge cinema industry, the British have a cultural fight on their hands to stop American English taking over. And it is not just the accent that some see as improper. Expressions such as 'speaking *with* someone' (as opposed to '*to*' them), 'Monday *thru*' Friday' (as opposed to '*till*') and the omission of prepositions as in 'I spoke with John Tuesday', are creeping into everyday parlance and so are reflected in the media as they will be. But there are no hard and fast rules; some will be resisted even by young people and some will pass through. If you are American broadcasting in Britain – you will have to be sensitive to this, as I am sure you already are.

Being culturally sensitive and aware of what is acceptable on the media of a certain country not only applies to Britain. If you have lived in a country in the Anglophone world different from your origin for any length of time the chances are that your accent will have changed towards being more like that of those around you. And that change will bode well for your broadcasting experience too.

SUMMARY

1. Varied intonation used naturally in conversation must be harnessed for presentation.
2. Experiment with pitch, pace and other techniques of vocal variety to find colour and range to add interest.
3. Breathing correctly is essential for all professional speakers. Exercises will give you more breath to control your output.
4. Relaxation and 'centre-ing' exercises will enhance your performance as will good posture.
5. Nerves can be controlled to be made to work for you. There are ways of keeping them in control.
6. It is good to warm up the voice. Use my suggestions or find more in other suggested voice books.
7. Some vocal problems you can solve but there also those you do not need to.
8. Accents are good to hear – they bring variety to the media. But think clarity and cultural sensitivity.

Your audience 4

CONNECTING WITH YOUR AUDIENCE

Awareness of the audience is more difficult and consequently more important for the TV and radio presenter than for the presenter whose audience is in front of him/her, who needs no reminder of their presence and behaviour. But how do you connect with an audience you cannot see? If you talk just to the camera or microphone – which might be a temptation since that is all that is in front of you (give or take a technician or some equipment) – then your audience will perceive you as if you were just talking to the lectern. You have to give them the impression that you have eye contact with them, otherwise they will do what they do if you were actually in front of them and not looking directly at them: they will become inattentive. You need to talk to the person beyond the microphone, through the camera lens. You need to engage them. And the imagination is useful here.

One of the significant differences between presentation to an audience physically in front of you and media presentation is that with the former you are aware of the group in front of you as a group: how many of them, what sort of people, if they are listening attentively. Via the media, by contrast, it is not useful to be aware of the thousands or millions. Imagine what an audience of 100,000 looks like – then imagine how you would speak to them if they were in front of you. This would not help your TV or radio presentation skills. Not being able to see the audience gives the advantage of being able to talk to them individually.

Engaging with your audience will benefit you in a number of ways. If you manage to make your delivery sound like a conversation you are having with one person with whom you have eye contact then you can see (or visualise) that person taking in what you are telling them and it will affect the way you talk to them. How ever many thousands or millions there are watching or listening to you, you will engage them all the better if you treat them as individual listeners and viewers. It will slow you down if you are nervous, and will allow the audience to digest the information you are telling them, just as in a real one-to-one conversation.

Where are your audience?

It is a good idea to think about where your viewers' television set is. In the living room on a shelving unit? In the kitchen perhaps or in the bedroom on a wall-stand with your viewer(s) watching you from their bed? Then you can address them there! It might seem odd to be situated, as it were, in the upper corner of someone's bedroom but you need to make contact with your viewer and if you imagine yourself talking to them from their set then you will achieve an effective, connecting, engaging communication, and will gain their attention.

Where the set is and where your viewers are can change according to what you are telling them. If you are presenting a cookery show then perhaps you should think of telling a woman in her kitchen. (Yes, I know it is politically incorrect and a stereotype but the guardians of such ethics cannot police your imagination and you have only to ask if it works or not.) Perhaps you are doing your cookery show for young urban male professionals who are watching you on a computer screen as they work. How will that change your presentation? Where you put your audience is part of *whom* you, the programme and even the channel are trying to reach. Your imagination becomes part of the marketing strategy since if you place your viewer/listener in the right place and you can keep their attention, then the advertisers can sell them the right products. Even if your channel is non-commercial the audience figures will keep your programme on the air.

EXERCISE

Take a neutral piece of presentational copy – a news story, any piece of journalistic narrative, something preferably written to be spoken rather than for the print media. Imagine where your audience is and address them there:

1. The living room relaxing on the sofa in front of the TV.
2. In the bedroom – they are in bed and you are on a dressing table or a stand higher up on the wall.
3. The kitchen – on the radio, so they will be doing some thing else while listening to you – or on TV and they will glance at you as a break from cooking.
4. On the car radio. They are driving.

Start with one location then change to another and notice how that affects the way you talk to your audience and tell your story.

VISUALISING YOUR AUDIENCE

Broadcasters often talk about visualising a certain person to help them get their message across. They talk to this ghost to engage their audience more effectively. It is certainly a technique which helps get you beyond the microphone or camera. And with radio especially it reinforces the feeling that you are talking to one person as in a conversation. But it does not work for everyone. Presenters must find their own way of connecting with their audience and often use their own variation of visualising their audience instead of merely copying a technique which in its most general form has become a cliché.

Some variations

Close relatives

There are those who imagine they are talking to their mother. If you have a mother and she loves you then she will probably already be listening to or watching you whether you imagine her to be or not. And because she loves you she may not be the most critical of listener/viewers. She is going to like what you are doing whatever you do. And that goes for partners and close relatives. They may not always like what you do, but what about their actual feedback? Is that helpful? They may tell you that you have a cold coming or that you sounded or looked tired this morning. Of course this may not affect the way you talk to them in your mind's eye as you present, but if they give you feedback it may well influence your presentation. And not everyone gets on with their close relations and may visualise them as over-critical.

Friends

A friend might be more suitable. But be aware that part of this process is seeing how people react when you tell them certain things. If your friend is particularly opinionated then their reaction might be out of step with what the majority of your listeners are thinking when you tell them a particular thing. It might represent one section of your audience. Will that influence the way you present? You need to keep a balance and bear in mind your audience may have a wide variety of opinions on certain topics, only one of which is represented by your friend.

Representative of audience

Imagine an acquaintance then, or someone who is from the demographic that is targeted by your programme output. But then there could be a problem with that too, since an imagined person from the demographic is a perception of the kind of person listening or watching but not a real person and so you could be tempted to patronise them because you think you know how they are made up: aged 25 to 40, middle-class, female, married, two children, at home, part-time job, middle-income... sounds very bland and certainly not a real person. Nevertheless it may work for you and there's only one way to find out.

EXERCISE

Again take a piece of neutral broadcast copy – news or feature material. Have two or three people in mind. Acquaintances will work best, rather than closer friends or relatives. Try to choose people for their differences from each other in gender, race, age, social class etc. Now read your material to them – visualising each in turn. Devote a couple of sentences to each one and notice how they might react to what you are telling them. If they are different then their reactions will be different and so also will be the way you tell them the information. If you record yourself doing this, you may notice the difference in your delivery as you move from one to another.

RADIO LISTENERS

What are they doing?

Listeners are often doing something else while they have the radio on: getting up in the morning, driving and eating are popular. If they are reading then their attention will be divided and you will be battling for some of it. Some go to sleep with the radio on. And some prefer talk to music when falling asleep. While broadcasting overnight at the BBC World Service people I knew (living in the UK) sometimes got in touch telling me that they had heard me at three in the morning. They had been listening to 'Book at Bedtime' (Radio 4 at 11 pm) and woken up to me telling them about the latest political developments in Azerbaijan (Radio 4 in the UK is taken over by World Service overnight on some frequencies). I asked them why they were listening at that time – they told me that they found the sound of speech comforting and that it helped them to sleep. Like a child being read to at night, they had dropped off.

Talking to them

Nevertheless whatever your listeners are doing you need to engage them, even if they end up going to sleep on you! The register is that of a conversation – one where only you are speaking – but one that is more intimate than that used to address a gathering. And though sometimes formal, as with news, the delivery is still as if one-to-one, to maximise comprehension by the listener. If you sound like you are reading it (which of course you often are) then it will sound less immediate. The listener will feel it is in some way second-hand, that the script is something they could read for themselves. They need to feel that you are telling them first-hand. The listener does not want a literary experience – they don't want to hear the punctuation – they just want the information.

To create the right relationship with your radio listener (remember they generally listen individually), you should be the correct distance from them – just as in a conversation. You should be only a little nearer the microphone than you imagine you are from your listener. You can imagine that s/he is just across the radio mic from you. If, as those late-night deejays are sometimes prone to do, you wanted to talk more intimately to the listener, you would lower your voice and move closer in to the mic. That is inappropriate for most programming, but it gives you an idea of how you can control the relationship you have with your listener.

Television viewers

Television never stops changing and neither do viewing habits. A great deal has happened in the TV industry since there were only two terrestrial channels on offer in the evening 50 years ago. Because there is so much choice depending on where they are, how they receive it and how they pay for it, the different audiences are perhaps more definable. Their habits are different from what they used to be.

Time it was when streets and bars emptied at a particular time of the evening for a popular show; then came the video recorder. There have been more innovations since then involving satellites, cables and digital boxes to name three hardware stories. How has this left the presenter and their relationship with the audience? I would have to say, little changed.

Viewers can zap you with the remote, but if the increased choice they have focusses the station or network more specifically on whom it is appealing to, then that will be your concern too as presenter. In the end that can make your task easier: you will know better whom you are trying to attract.

Outside broadcasts

Sometimes there are more than just you and your listener or viewer. Outside broadcasts take the audience with you and interviews and vox pops allow them to share your experience of telling your story through other people and places. But wherever you are you need to keep the audience in mind. They must always figure in your broadcast, whether you are asking questions of an interviewee, or are on radio describing a scene that you are experiencing. Occasionally you hear the audience being excluded from a conversation on air, for example when two presenters share a private joke. That is definitely a turn-off: always include your audience or they will exclude you!

On-air identity

Sometimes presenters are asked why, in real life, they don't sound or look like they do on the media, and you need to ask yourself the same question. Why do you have a different voice for broadcasting? Why do you look different on the screen? The difference is more marked on radio since people imagine what you look like from your voice and are then surprised when you do not look like that. But even on TV they are surprised, partly because you do not belong in the street or on the bus – you belong on the box in their living room.

If you are a newsreader then the formality of the news will prevent you from sounding like you do with your friends in conversation. The material will affect your sound however conversational you manage to make it.

With any programme you create an on-air identity, which will necessarily be different from your real identity. It will be one that allows you to get information over and do the job you need to do whether it is presenting a music show, being funny, being a news and current affairs anchor, being the presenter or a studio guest on a daytime TV show, or whatever. Hopefully the difference between you, and 'on-air' you, will be subtle, which will nevertheless surprise people who meet you in real life if only because they will experience you in a situation that is not doing any of those jobs and so will be remarkable for them. But your on-air identity will be no less powerful for being as near as you can make it to your normal persona.

INTERACTION

As with all presentation the more contact and interaction you have with your audience the stronger their engagement and consequently the stronger the identity you will have. You will get to know each other, or rather you will have that impression, as indeed they will too. You may be surprised by the familiarity some of your audience begin to adopt when addressing themselves to you in emails, texts or by post and on the phone.

Discussions with the audience

Interactivity is important and becoming more so. Where you can see or hear the presenter interacting with the audience on shows devoted to that relationship it is self-evident. There are, of course, skills associated with dealing with the public and discussing issues with them. Presenters need to be well briefed on the subject of the programme in order to attempt to extract a balanced bunch of opinions from a studio audience for example. You must be able to probe and manage the audience.

News and current affairs programmes

Interactivity is becoming more evident in news and current affairs programmes nowadays, with presenters canvassing opinion from their audience. Emails and texts are the usual form of audience contact with a selection of opinions being read out on air. This gives the programme a feeling that the producers are taking into consideration the concerns of the audience, that they lack arrogance and that they are accessible. They may well produce new angles and issues not thought of by the journalists, and throw up questions for politicians and other guests hitherto not considered. There is evidence of this going further with dedicated current affairs programmes entirely devoted to interaction and audience contribution.

Phone-ins

The phone-in programme provides the presenter with direct contact with the audience. To some listeners the presenter seems to be a friend – someone they know. If you have built up expectations in your audience you have also broken down barriers. You are now speaking directly to your audience and the conversation is actual between you and your listeners rather than virtual. But there are drawbacks, and you need to become skilled in managing some callers. If you are discussing a controversial subject then you will have opinionated, aggressive even bigoted callers. Some may know more than you about the topic. Some presenters adopt a robust tone themselves to get things going and think nothing of dumping a caller and moving on to the next. This often has the effect of making the programme more edgy and therefore interesting to listen to, whether you agree with the presenter or their respondents or not.

In the end it is an editorial, even a channel/station decision of how to handle the audience and what tone to take with them.

SUMMARY

1. Connect with the audience by speaking beyond the camera or mic.
2. Speak to the audience as individuals.
3. Where are they when they are viewing or listening?
4. Visualise an acquaintance – notice how they take in what you are telling them.
5. What are your radio listeners doing while listening to you?
6. Changing TV technology does not change your relationship with the audience.
7. Interactivity with the audience is good for the programme, and good for your on-air identity.

Your material 5

'It's not how you say it, it's what you say'

This has become a favourite slogan of mine to encourage trainees to focus on the material. The reason it is not about how you say it is not because how you say it does not matter – of course it does – it is because as soon as you focus on how you are saying it rather than what you are saying, it will become all about how you are saying it rather than what you are saying; and that will weaken your message and in the end, therefore, also how you deliver it. Stay focussed on the message and how you deliver it will effectively look after itself.

Let's look at some material.

News

News presentation would seem an easy ride to some perhaps since you have the text in front of you either on autocue for TV or a script for radio, and it's just a question of reading it. But if that is what you do that is what it will sound like – read – and your audience will quickly switch off, if not the channel, then their attention. The trick is to tell the news not read it so that you engage your audience. In the telling of it you need therefore to know what it is about, and what has come before i.e. the context of the news. During the aftermath of the Iraq war, if Baghdad had been a peaceful city then a bomb going off in the city centre killing 30 people would have been a different story from the one which was, alas, an all too frequent news story then. It must be read knowing the frequency with which these incidents occur.

Reading comprehension

You need to know what you are talking about. It will naturally colour what you read.

In the following sentence you can see how a newsreader's comprehension of the story is important. The story dates from 2005:

> *'Dominique de Villepin is in London for talks with the prime minister. Meanwhile the French foreign minister is in Washington for the NATO conference.'*

If you stress 'French' then it indicates that you don't know that Dominique de Villepin is French and maybe you thought he was the foreign minister of another country. If you stress all three words equally – 'French foreign minister'– it indicates you do not know who Dominique de Villepin is; only if you stress the single word 'foreign' does the audience understand that Dominique de Villepin is not only French but probably the French Prime Minister and importantly the audience realises that you know that too.

Context

Because the presenter needs to engage with his/her material, not only is preparation important with news but also understanding and experience: the more knowledgeable you are about news the more comprehensible your presentation of it will be. With understanding and experience you can put the news into context. There is a reason why newsreaders tend nowadays to be news journalists rather than announcers. They are involved in the writing and compiling of the news, not just the speaking of it.

If you give an actor the news to read you will hear someone lifting the information off the page, not just 'reading' it; but it will sound strange because the chances are the actor will not have the experience to know the background to the news and so you will not hear the context.

Context is what is between the lines. It is the background; the unspoken common knowledge about a subject which links the presenter, the audience and the material. Most news stories are developments of established stories. They refer to information already known. This needs to be acknowledged by the presenter. It will make communication easier if the presenter and news writer can accurately assess what the audience already knows of a story. You may give some background to a story but you want to focus on what is new.

When there is a complicated story it is not unusual for the audience to feel they have missed something and so cannot follow the latest developments as well as they might. I know I have felt this about some stories. Sometimes there is a need to bring people up-to-date with a story by repeating information some will already know or by explaining a complicated or specialist story, at the expense of losing some people in the process. It has to be an informed calculation. There is also more space for background and explanation in current affairs programmes.

CURRENT AFFAIRS

Programmes devoted to news stories and their background depend on their material for their worth. But the management of the material is the challenge and that partly becomes the responsibility of the presenter and their journalistic ability literally to present the story. It may be the angle on the stories and the quality of the guests rather than substantial information that attract the audience. Current affairs programmes assume the audience's interest in current events and their wish to see news stories from new perspectives. Controversially such programmes also increasingly seek to entertain.

Information or entertainment?

If we, as the audience, look at why we go to news and current affairs programmes as frequently as we do (if we do), we are surely not only after the latest new stories: we are looking also for extended coverage of stories that we already know about. And we are after debate and clarification. We want people in power questioned and challenged perhaps by politicians as well as journalists. We want to see accountability in action. We want to see motives challenged. Why go to war? Why is public money being spent on a particular project? Why and how are public services failing, and indeed whether they are, etc. Such is the stuff of day-to-day current affairs journalism. And that goes beyond informing us. Perhaps we like to see politicians humiliated by a vicious interviewer. Perhaps we want to see how someone copes after a tragedy, a criminal brought to justice or a celebrity misbehaving. Current affairs broadcasting in the UK is becoming more tabloid and consequently is moving closer to entertainment.

The presenter as journalist

The current affairs presenter must therefore be able to provide for those audience needs and can only do this through a thorough knowledge of the material and a journalistic nose for how to focus on a productive and interesting angle. You may have to do this in an interview or debate. But you will certainly have to do it in the simple presentation of the material. And your ability to write well comes in here. You cannot present the story without involving yourself in creating it. Having done that, you own it – it becomes yours; the audience will now relate to the story through your observation of it. Thus who presents is crucial: you are in a position of power. Audiences come to the current affairs programme for the presenter's way of dealing with the stories, as much as for the stories themselves.

The journalist who is not a specialist will find their on-air identity through their journalistic style. If they are investigative, for instance, they will develop a style demanded of that kind of enquiry. In documentary film the story may be told by means of interviews and choice of clips where the presenter is necessarily doing the job of finding the facts in less than co-operative environments. In doing that job the presentation will look after itself. News presenters and interviewers are well known for their no-nonsense, sometimes pugnacious, personas. It helps the audience to identify a style but it comes with the material. You simply cannot interview a shifty politician as if you were doing a women's health programme. The presentation here again comes back to the material.

The radio breakfast show

The breakfast show is a popular slot on radio (and to a lesser extent on TV) for current affairs programming because of its wide-ranging treatment of the day's news stories. Editors of breakfast shows may be very selective in their material which may sometimes be trivial. Breakfast shows – typically 6 am to 9 am – attract the highest radio audiences of the day, and rely heavily on their presenters, who are generally proportionally better paid than their colleagues.

The breakfast show sets the agenda and analyses the breaking stories with live interviews and discussions, sometimes in a fast-moving and busy schedule which may include music, packages (or mini-features), outside broadcasts and live phone interviews. In order to manage such material breakfast presenters must be able to deal with a lot of different kinds of material which may have only been available earlier that day or overnight or may break during the programme! They will have scanned all the papers by the time the show starts and have some ideas of how they want to treat some of the stories they are going to focus on. They need a lot of energy which is fuelled by adrenaline sometimes to the point of mania. A successful breakfast show host displays wide-ranging general knowledge of news and trivia, has charm and personality and importantly is able to get up at 3 am and perform at 6 am for three hours, up to five days a week!

FEATURE PROGRAMMES

Often presenters and guests in feature programmes, such as those about history or gardening for instance, will be specialists (historians or gardeners) first and broadcasters second. But even if you already have expertise in your subject you may need to brush up on your presentation technique. If you are an infrequent guest on radio and TV programmes you may need to think about how well you are getting your expertise over. In general the more you are exposed to the media, to the producers and other professionals who will comment on your presentation, the better the presentation of your material will become.

Who are you talking to?

You will need to think about what material suits your perceived audience. If it is too complicated you will have to modify it to make it more palatable. But by how much? If you go too far in this process you may seem patronising. You have to judge the audience and write sensitively. And bear in mind what pleases one may annoy another: in some cases problems are unavoidable. I have seen and heard doctors and economists go too far when using metaphor and simile: 'The heart is like a Swiss clockmaker's most ingenious invention...but after a while even with his most intricately designed model some of the cogs may need attention or even replacement.' Or: 'the Chancellor is on a voyage where having met rough weather he may have wished his boat was propelled by powerful outboard motors rather than the wind in the canvas he set sail with.' Go to *Private Eye* magazine for amusing examples of silly journalese.

What is the story?

You have to gauge the audience but you must immerse yourself in the subject first and decide what the story is about. This is quite simply a journalistic exercise which you may decide with your editor but is essential to best presentation. Some journalists/presenters write the title and cue to their story before they start the investigative and research process in order to remind themselves of what the story is about at every stage of their work and prevent any possibility of getting bogged down or wandering off on tangents.

Presenter as role model

And what of women's programmes, health, holiday, children's, sport, lifestyle and the endless chocolate-box assortment which makes up not only the hours of air time now available but the numerous dedicated cable and digital channels? Producers and executives have firm ideas of who they want to front their programmes and channels, and who they want as guests (which is why you see the same people coming up again and again). And if you ask yourself why would programme editors choose a middle-aged woman journalist rather than a young male doctor to front their health show, you may get some idea by thinking about the audience they are likely to attract. Nevertheless that journalist/presenter had better know her stuff or she will lose credibility. Equally the doctor may have found it difficult to interpret clinical language for the layperson, which would also have been a failing.

Know your stuff

If you are presenting or being a guest on a programme in a subject area you are new to, or know too little about, you must do your research and make sure you are as familiar as you can be with what the station, channel or programme does – if it is on the air already – and what similar output is doing, if it is not. Whatever the programme or channel you will need to be as informed as possible about the content to do a credible job and there can be no short cuts or excuses for not doing some hard work.

BEING AN EXPERT

You may be invited on to a programme as a guest or be interviewed on the basis of your knowledge of a particular subject. You may be an academic, enthusiast, professional or for any reason knowledgeable about the subject in the programme. As an expert you may already have contact with non-experts and be used to giving advice to those who know less about your field than you do, and so be used to explaining, making plain and presenting in lay terms – in short – communicating your subject matter to others.

Focus on your message and your audience

It is nevertheless important that you prepare. Be clear what you want to say. Make sure you have the arguments you want to put over clearly described, logical and in the right order. Ask yourself what you are trying to say. Keep it simple and try not to cram in too much information.

Think about who you are talking to. Here again you may like to visualise a particular person you are telling the information to. If you are practised at explaining your expertise to people, think about how you do that on a one-to-one basis (rather than lecturing a large audience), and engage your audience that way. You may be telling a presenter the information in response to questions (and we will be dealing with interviewing in later chapters). You will always have to engage the audience and the best way to do that is to show your enthusiasm for your subject. In the end your enthusiasm rather than your knowledge will endear you to your audience, even though what you know is important for you to be able to select the right material.

You will get a feeling for when your material goes across and when it fails to. You will develop an antenna for communication. Remember that anecdote and example help get information across and the audience will retain it longer if they are helped by illustration. In this way you are operating in the same way as speakers to a live audience. But remember the intimacy of media communication.

WRITING FOR BROADCAST

The basis for good presentation is a well-written script. How much writing you do will depend on what kind of programme you are presenting. If you can ad-lib, or semi-script links then you may not need a script. Perhaps you can rely on others to write, in which case you will be adept at lifting others' copy off the page. A newsreader may have to stick rigidly to the script but if it is you who wrote it then you will presumably, as a journalist, already know how to write well. But for broadcast? Let's look at some basics.

Writing for speech

A presentation script should be written as it is spoken. When we speak we use short forms, and the punctuation is not as it is in literary English. When we speak in conversation we do not think about commas and full stops and sentences but rather lumps of information. That said, a news script has its own formality and must contain a lot of information. So the writing will depend on what it is that is to be presented. One rule of thumb however is that if it is to be written for speech it should be spoken out loud as it is being written. Only that way can you hear what it sounds like and you will avoid writing combinations of words that are difficult to speak. At a more subtle level you can hear what your ideas and information sound like, which may well change the way you write.

You should also bear in mind that text for speech and broadcast gives the audience only one opportunity to take in the information. They cannot (or do not even if they can) review it as they can and do with print copy (e.g. in newspapers, magazines and books).

Example: print copy vs. broadcast copy

Have a look at and compare these two pieces of news journalism. One is from the print media and the other from the broadcast media. One is intended for the eye and one for the ear. The latter is what concerns us here as presenters.

> *Print copy*
> 'Serb nationalists destroyed two checkpoints on Kosovo's new border with Serbia yesterday, causing NATO troops to intervene for the first time since the split from Belgrade.'
>
> *Broadcast copy*
> 'Serbs protesting at Kosovo's declaration of independence have attacked two border crossings in the north of the country. NATO peacekeepers have been deployed to curb the violence.'

The first taken from a newspaper just does not read as well out loud as the second taken from a radio newsroom. The second is more direct and it has two sentences which makes it an easier read. It is not so much that you need plenty of breath in the first to get through the sentence, it is difficult to maintain the momentum and sense till the end. The information is clear in both versions. The second is readable out loud.

EXERCISE

Take a piece of material that you have written for reading rather than speech – an email, letter or text for example – about six or seven lines. Turn it into a script for speech. Read it out. Compare it with the original. Now take a paragraph from a newspaper or magazine (not written to be read out loud), read it out and notice how difficult it can be to get off the page. Now rewrite it for speech, and read it out again.

JOURNALISM

Whether or not you have ambitions in journalism, as communicators on radio and TV you can learn a lot from journalists. Those, for instance, who are interviewed by journalists can learn to communicate and answer their questions better by understanding what the journalist wants and how s/he operates. Part of understanding journalists and how they work is to try to understand whom they are writing for – their audience. Journalists make information palatable to their perceived consumers. And that skill is a very useful one for those who appear on radio and TV.

Journalists can teach presenters the way. Thinking about the material and how much interest it will provoke in your audience becomes an essential if instinctive skill. It will stand you in good stead, not only in the presenting of it, but in forging that all-important relationship with your audience and giving them what will interest them.

SUMMARY

1. 'It's the material, stupid.' Not *how* but *what*.
2. News needs context. Tell it rather than read it.
3. Information and entertainment – both are required of current affairs and feature programmes.

4. Presenting expertise: think about the audience and how much help they need in understanding the material.
5. Write for speech, not for reading.
6. Think like a journalist.

Reading a script

6

Turning the written word for the eye into the spoken word for the ear is a technique that will be useful to you in several media situations. It is a technique that people approach differently. But by whatever means, you will need to find a way of transforming written text into intelligible and fluent speech.

IS THE SCRIPT NECESSARY?

Why have a script? Surely the best broadcasting or presenting happens when people are just themselves and tell it rather than read it. I think you should 'tell' it, and when it is done well that is maybe what it looks or sounds like, told not read. But certain material has to be scripted, and read – for different reasons.

Information

The news needs to be carefully scripted and broadcast exactly as it is written. The material has to be accurate, laden with information and carefully crafted by news journalists. Cues to features and packages, although offering a little more leeway, also contain essential information and need to be read closely, keeping to the text.

Most radio and TV journalism whether hard news, feature or speciality programming, requires tight scripting for informational, timing and technical reasons. If it sounds as though the presenter is making it up as they go along, then they are doing their job well.

Timing

Both TV and radio broadcast scripts often need to be read to time – that is, fitted exactly into an allocated time slot. Voice over video needs to be read exactly as written for timing purposes, since the words must fit the pictures. Also for timing purposes radio and TV continuity often needs to be carefully crafted, although you can develop a technique that allows you not to script but fill the time slot by accurately ad-libbing.

Advertising

Voice-overs for commercials are very carefully written. Highly paid agency copywriters may have been working a long time to get exactly the right nuance they are looking for, and the voice-over needs to respect that by reading the words as written.

Technical necessities

Because of the technical obligations in radio and especially TV, others need to know what is going to be said before those in front of the mic or camera say it. Camera operators for instance, the director, vision mixers, studio managers playing audio into a programme, all depend on cues to do their job. The script is for them too.

There are of course unscripted programmes or parts of programmes. Deejays, for instance, do not tend to work from a script although I sometimes advise them to semi-script their links especially if they have a lot of information to get over between music. The next chapter on ad-libbing has more on this.

What scripts look like

For some the very look of a script can be daunting. It is important to understand why a script looks as it does and whom it is for.

Radio scripts

Radio scripts look more like ordinary typed sheets. But they have other information: durations for example (how long in minutes and seconds); they may contain information on audio from other sources (e.g. music from CD or audio storage, phone line, speech from storage) that will be played in. As with TV this information is necessary for the producer and studio manager who craft and operate the programme. Even if the presenter is on their own in the studio (self-op), operating the equipment as well as reading, the script contains essential information other than the text:

EXAMPLE OF A RADIO SCRIPT

<u>Q BABY</u> **<u>Duration 1'05"</u>**

Police investigating the death of a three year old boy in a fire in a house in Manchester have arrested the boy's mother. Jane Smith – who's 21 – told the police that she was knocked unconscious by intruders who she said started the fire. Another man who was arrested in connection with the fire has now been released on bail. Our Manchester correspondent Jim Brown reports:

AUDIO Brown/Baby/119623

IN: 'Jane Smith…

OUT: …being able to care for her child.'

DUR: 23"

BACK ANNO

Jim Brown. This is the second death of a child in a fire in Manchester in a week. The city's fire service has issued a statement calling for more vigilance to prevent fires in the home.

Notation

- Q' refers to cue.
- 'AUDIO Brown/baby/119623' refers to the clip from audio store with its title and reference number.
- 'IN' denotes the first words of the audio clip.
- 'OUT' the last ones.
- 'DUR' is the duration of the clip (23 seconds).
- 'Back Anno' means back announcement (i.e. after the clip).

TV scripts

Television scripts are usually divided so that the vision is on the left with voice text on the right. When you are voicing over pictures it is useful to know what is on the screen and how long you have for the text if the vision source is timed. The producer, director and camera all need to refer to the script. It is as much for them as the presenter.

The following script is a typical example with text on the right for the presenter and information on the left for the gallery. The presenter will be reading the first sentence off autocue as he is in vision; he will be able to read the part of the script for the voice-over (OOV or 'out of vision') off computer or hard copy while he is out of vision. The film clip is 15 seconds – the script is timed to cover the clip. It is for live transmission.

EXAMPLE OF A TV SCRIPT

```
30 SUITCASE-TX-SUITCASE 060308 OOV 1330   Look West

[Live Read: Pres in Vis]

    The Jury has retired to consider its verdict
    in the case of a cleaner accused of murdering
    her employer and dumping her body in a field
    in Oxfordshire.

[AUTOMATION: CLIP\PRA
SUITCASE OOV (DJC602130)
\MANUAL
IN WORDS: (LIVE OOV)
OUT WORDS:
ITEM TIME: 0'15"]
[TECH LAST SHOT CHANGE AT: 0'06"]
[CG at 0'01": LOCATOR 2006
\Milton Common, nr Thame\]

    (OOV) The charred remains of the body and
    suitcase were found at Milton Common near
    Thame by farm workers in July last year. The
    dead woman was identified as Theresa Browning
    from London. Her cleaner Yolanda Kowski from
    Ealing denies killing her.
```

Notation

- The top line contains the title of the piece, the programme number, reference to an out-of-vision live delivery by the presenter, the time of transmission and the name of the programme.
- The first section on the right is read by the presenter in vision off the autocue.
- The second section on the right is read out of vision.
- The information on the left refers to the title and reference of the film clip in storage, the duration and a reference to the last shot change in the clip.

Timing notation

A single inverted comma usually denotes minutes, and double inverted commas seconds; so 2'35" means 2 minutes and 35 seconds. There are other systems which also include hours, but this notation is often used for more common, shorter pieces.

PREPARATION

There are those who sight-read well and are so proud of their talent that they sometimes prefer not to see the script beforehand. But no matter how experienced and engaging the reader is, a sight-read script lacks something. To be able to do a good job on a script you need to understand how the ideas are communicated through the words in order to give it depth and too anticipate what is coming up.

Pre-reading

Reading the script out loud before you present it is essential for a good performance. Only as you hear it out loud can you tell what it is going to sound like 'on the night'. Certain combinations of words which look fine on the page do not sound so good when they are read out: these can be identified and changed, for instance unintentional alliteration which can unnecessarily distract the audience.

You should aim to find the 'soul' of the text so that you can represent it as you focus on what the text is trying to get over. You may be familiar with the material in which case you can make sure that the script really does do what it is meant to – get the information and ideas across effectively, concisely and clearly. It is surprising how confused some writing can be. Getting to the sense can involve a discussion with others (including the writer if you did not write it yourself) to try to find the best expression of the content. It is often good to discuss it since it is then in the open – spoken, public, rather than internal, personal or still part of the intellectual processes of one person.

You will be aware of how well written the script is as you read it out loud. A well-written script feels like it 'reads itself'. It comes off the page – you do not have to work hard at it. It is easy to read. It gets the information across, is clear and sounds good in speech. Good writers of scripts for presentation write for speech, so that it immediately works as such.

Pronunciations

Tricky pronunciations should be researched and practised. Wrong pronunciation will undermine your whole performance as the audience will judge you if you mispronounce words they consider to be common knowledge. And the only way not to be caught out is to see them before broadcast. Proper names and foreign words and names need to be researched even if they are unfamiliar to a local audience. If you mispronounce a foreign place or VIP then you will lose credibility. I once pronounced Waco (Texas) 'whacko' (instead of 'way-co') since it was the first time I had seen it. To a North American audience this mistake is laughable not only because it is a commonly known place in the US, but also because 'whacko' means crazy in modern American vernacular.

It is important that you rehearse a difficult or foreign name in context since often long or difficult non-English names disrupt the normal rhythm of an English sentence, and you need to fit it into the phrase. One common fault is that the presenter gets the name right but then somehow the rest of the sentence goes awry. It would be better to get the name wrong but keep the sense of the sentence.

If the name is long then divide it up. The first time I came across the capital of Madagascar, Antananarivo, I felt I had put too many 'nana's in there. Divided up it is not so difficult: 'anta nana reevoo' with the stress on the 'ree' and the last 'o' is pronounced long: 'oo' so it sounds like 'untunanareevoo' when said at speed with the only stress on the 'ee'. However it should be practised in context i.e. using the whole sentence so that you get used to the rhythm. Try the sentence:

> `'The two rival candidates in Madagascar's presidential election will meet in the capital Antananarivo today in a bid to calm tension after earlier clashes.'`

GETTING IT OFF THE PAGE

When you read a script (whether or not you have written it), you need to be able to lift it off the page; to turn it into speech; to tell it; to make it your own. If it sounds read, the listener becomes aware of the script rather than the information it contains. And they become aware of your struggle to communicate it, which will act as a barrier to the flow. How then can you effectively get the words off the page and turn the written into the spoken word?

Variety of intonation

An inexperienced reader is faced with two familiar problems: sounding monotonous on the one hand or sing-song on the other. Producers and listeners comment on these as common faults. More often still, readers criticise their own performances on playback as having either insufficient or inappropriate variety. Not enough emphasis or colour, or stress on the wrong words. There are several ways of dealing with these problems.

Too much and/or inappropriate variety

Inexperienced presenters try to add interest to their delivery by giving strong emphasis to certain words. Sometimes it is out of fear of sounding monotonous or in an effort to reach a young audience whom they perceive to pay attention only to arresting delivery. But if the emphasis is inappropriate then the sense will be sacrificed which rather defeats the object. I have heard newsreaders and presenters emphasise every fourth word (as if given advice to do such) in an effort to inject energy into a script. Look at the following:

> 'The rock band **U2**, have won a **legal** battle with the **band's** former stylist - over their **lead** singer Bono's cowboy **hat**. Lola Cashman claimed **she'd** been given the **Stetson** in 1987 - along **with** a pair of **earrings**, a sweatshirt **and** a pair of trousers. The High **Court** in Dublin has **now** ordered her to **return** them.'

I haven't picked out exactly every fourth word but I have heard this kind of delivery (emphasising the words in bold), and of course it makes it very difficult to understand. The presenter thinks it makes it urgent and immediate and therefore attractive to a younger audience fed on a diet of music and sounds and not too much talk. There may also be music on a track behind the speech which makes it even more difficult for the listener to understand.

Other sing-song deliveries come about where the comprehension of the text is sacrificed to an attempt to colour the delivery. Some examples are given in the section on 'Intonation' in Chapter 3. It generally happens when the presenter is focussing more on *how* rather than *what* they are saying.

Monotonous delivery

Few people speak monotonously. There are exceptions and often when people are giving information which they may find boring they may consequently give a monotonous delivery. However when a reader is monotonous it is usually because they cannot lift it off the page. They are stuck with the text as text. They cannot bring to life. It is true that some text is difficult to breathe life into, and if you are struggling then you need to do your homework on the information that is in the text. Ask yourself what the text is about. And tell it to the audience. Find the voice that speaks in real life – use that as a starting point – and make the text your own.

Most problems with reading a script are caused by not relating to its content. And monotony is no exception. If you are not interested in what you are reading, then you will have an uphill task. It is essential that it engages you, otherwise it will not engage your audience. It may sound obvious but the best way not to sound boring is not to be bored. If the material excites you – if you can even find a passion for it – then your delivery will be informed and the audience engaged.

EXERCISE

Take a piece of text (news or any other copy written for broadcast): study it, pre-read it and record it. Put the text aside. Now tell the story in your own words answering the imaginary question: what is this story about? (still recording). Finally read and record the text again informed by your new understanding of it. When you listen back, notice particularly the difference between the first two recordings, between the first text reading and you telling it in your own words. Hopefully this is how you speak in real life and it demonstrates a very natural use of intonation and variety that all of us use to communicate with each other. And some of that natural variety will hopefully have rubbed off on to the final reading.

However, merely sounding like you do in real life may not be enough for some to inject life and energy into a script. So we must go further, over the top even, without straying into the sing-song or inappropriate mode as shown above. We must find a situation in which you are obliged naturally to find plenty of variety. One that presents itself perhaps to some more than others is reading stories to children.

Reading children's stories

Children make a wonderful audience because of their honesty. They are either 100 per cent interested in what you are reading them or zero per cent. And they make this known to you. So you have a simple task on your hands when you attempt to engage them with your reading. How you do this often brings into play an urge to exaggerate the meaning of the words with intonation to stimulate and keep the interest of the child. It will perhaps remind you of what interested you when you were a child or assumptions (sometimes cruelly corrected by a child's disapproval) about what children like. You will dramatise the text to play to these interests. Your intonation will vary and you will take the words to the child, either with eye contact or quite natural projection, to keep their attention. Don't take my word for it. If you do not live with one, find a child and read them a story. You can even try reading them a presentation script and see how far you get with that. If you animate it with exaggerated emphasis you might get quite far before they give up on you!

Meaning-laden words and phrases

In the process of making sense of a script to an audience it is sometimes useful to sort out the phrases that carry the meaning and can therefore be given some extra recognition when delivering a text. This will necessarily relegate some words to secondary importance. This helps to vary the intonation, not for the sake of variety but in order to get the sense across in a more definitive way. Look at the following news story:

EXERCISE

'West Lancashire district council, has voted to ban its workers from taking cigarette breaks. Staff will be given help to give up but could face the sack if they don't comply with the new regulations which will be brought in next March.'

Read it and record it then underline the words and phrases which you think carry the meaning. Record it again. You will see my choice at the end of the chapter using bold to denote the meaning-laden words and phrases (see page 88). You can follow my choice if you like but it is better if you stick with your own, and see if it works, and the reading is improved. If it does not work then change your choice of the meaning-laden words.

Intonation transmits meaning

When delivering a script you should try to get the meaning over to your audience by conveying the ideas and information. This involves more than merely reading the words. It is as if, as in conversation, the words come as an effect of thinking about the ideas and information. In so doing, again as in free-form conversation, you will get the meaning across as much by intonation informed by your comprehension of the text, as by voicing and articulating the words on the page. We have all had the experience of hearing words without taking in the meaning and also of speaking them without comprehension, as if our brain is not connected to our ears or mouth. Through concentration on the 'what' (the subject of the text) it should be less possible to by-pass the meaning.

You can speak or hear lines of Shakespeare, even appreciating the metre and beauty of the words, without full comprehension, because of the archaic style. And yet how much more wonderful are those lines when the full meaning comes across, either because you have worked out the meaning or an actor has delivered them so well that their meaning is transmitted immediately.

Wrong intonation

You can see how intonation is affected by inappropriate use of punctuation, upper case, underline, bold, etc. as in the following:

EXERCISE

'West Lancashire DISTRICT council, has voted TO ban its **workers** from taking cigarette breaks staff will be; given help to give, up but could face the sack if they don't comply **with** the new regulations which, will be brought in **NEXT** March.'

Try reading it aloud.

It is difficult to make sense of this with such confusing use of punctuation, caps, underline and bold. It will affect the intonation. And the intonation is what the audience picks up to get the sense of what you are saying.

Intonation between familiars

Notice how, in a conversation between friends or family, meaning is conveyed more by intonation than is the case in formal, spoken communication. Such interlocutors use short form to by-pass formal communication. This is imitated by dialogue writers and actors in film and TV drama, especially those films which strive for realism. Sometimes film dialogue is difficult to understand, since we are witnessing the short form rather than taking part in it, and also the short form from one area of the Anglophone world is not easily understood in another. East Londoners may find film dialogue between Texans difficult to understand, but then Texans will have the same problem with cockney. This is not just because of the accent but because the speakers are picking up the meaning of what is being said by intonation.

Projection

Normally on the media we use the same volume level as we would in conversation with one or two others. Perhaps there is a certain heightening, especially if there are others in the studio with us. If there is a studio audience that is another matter and the presenter needs to relate to them as well as the 'folks at home'. However just as I have found it useful to go over the top and exaggerate to find flexibility in the voice (as with reading to children), so also is it useful to project, as if to a large audience, so that you can bring it back down again and yet use what you need when projecting to lift the text off the page.

Talking to a group

When addressing a group you are very aware of how the audience is reacting to what you are saying. If you have done any teaching you will recognise this. This reaction tends to change the delivery you give (or should do if you are hoping to keep their attention). You will need to make sure that all of the group can hear you so you speak up. But it is not just a matter of volume. Voice projection does what it says – projects the voice over a distance. It involves articulation in particular, but most of all awareness of whom you are talking to and how far away they are. Actors do it in the theatre and can even project whispers. Try this exercise:

EXERCISE

Put your hand a short distance in front of your mouth and talk to it. Say anything you like, as if you are talking to a friend, but it will be intimate (vocalised but little more than whispering), as your hand is only a short distance from your mouth. Continue talking to your hand but move it further away from you so you have to raise your voice a little. Then continue to talk but now to the other side of the room. Now talk beyond the room to somewhere down the corridor – about 20 metres away. Now bring it back into the room, to your hand and bring your hand back to your mouth. Notice what happens to your voice as you do this. It is not just about volume is it? You need flexibility and variety of tone to achieve this.

Having achieved projection you can now feel that you are talking to somebody as you read. You project the text to that person. It sometimes helps to lift the script in front of you as you talk beyond the microphone, on radio or TV voice-over, to the audience. If on camera you talk to them through the lens.

BREAKING DOWN THE SCRIPT

For some the script is a barrier whereas it should be an aid. It is your ordered thoughts. It is the material: what you need (and want) to express to your audience. It allows you to be articulate and logical. But it is also a lump of text on the page, and if it is long then you will need to break it down.

You can only hope that the writing keeps to short sentences. If you come across a long sentence then, if you cannot re-write it, you can treat it like several short sentences. You can easily do this in the reading, holding the clauses in your (and therefore the listener's) mind, as you come to the conclusion of the sentence. You do not need to rush or run out of breath. Take your time with it.

Paragraphs and other breaks

Paragraphs are one way of breaking the text and if you are writing the script for broadcast I would encourage you to write in short paragraphs. New paragraphs give you an opportunity to bring fresh energy to a new section. The audience will appreciate this too.

You can also use dots …… or dashes – which may be inappropriate for text only for the eye – but for reading it helps.

We do not speak in sentences with commas and full stops. We speak in lumps of information – bite-sized – which are easily digestible. But we do hear punctuation and therefore speak it. Exclamation or question marks, inverted commas, capital or italic letters can all be transmitted vocally and often are. You should be careful when reading a script with them in, unless that is what you want to transmit. They affect the intonation with the temptation for instance to emphasise highlighted words or phrases.

However such printing devices can be used to help delivery. Even if you only use a pencil, which is more practical if reading from hard copy, marking up your script can be helpful – but with a warning.

Marking up the script

Some presenters cover their scripts with markings; others leave them virgin. People do whatever works for them. There is no hard and fast rule. I tend to underline words which need attention for pronunciation and then put an accent (` or ´) over the syllable that needs emphasis in an unfamiliar word or name. I may also put a mark for timing purposes – and possible 'early outs' (or 'pots' as such are called), where I can finish the script before the end because of timing, and/or because the information left out is non-essential. I sometimes also use a linking elongated 'u' sign to signify that a sentence has not finished at the end of a line or on the bottom of the page, so that my attention will be drawn previously to its continuation on the next line or page.

However if you are working live and you get used to working with marked-up scripts then be prepared for working with a last-minute script which you have not had time to mark up. If you are dependent on your markings then it may throw you. I generally find too much marking draws my attention away from what the script is about. It is not about the words, it is about the ideas and information denoted by the words.

TALKING TO TIME

Much presentation involves respecting the clock. Radio and TV studios are full of clocks, and you will need to get used to noting the time (in minutes and seconds) precisely, as you read. Do not become dependent on either analogue or digital, since you will get both. You will also be cued by floor managers or studio managers visually or in your earpiece or headphones.

Words per second

As a rule of thumb we speak three words per second, and 14 lines per minute of normal A4 typescript with normal borders and alignment. I use 'normal' and 'rule of thumb' loosely since such timing judgements are not precise and often text has a computer-generated 'duration' which may over-rule this. Computer systems sometimes used for script-writing calculate words per second automatically and display it at the top of the script. But looking at a piece of text you can get an idea of its duration counting words or lines. Computer durations may be tweaked – and remember some people naturally speak quicker than others, so do not feel that these durations are hard and fast. I will happily add to or subtract from a computer duration if I feel it does not suit my natural speed.

Speed

Obviously how fast you speak impacts on how much text you can get into a timed slot. If you speak quickly (and well) then make sure you have enough text to fit the slot. But you should be able to be flexible so that you can speed up or slow down to fit the slot without it becoming obvious, so that the rhythm does not sound unnatural.

One technique

If you need to fit your text into an exact timing slot (which you often do) then you need to have some options. And the first one that comes to mind is the 'early out' – that is an optional finishing point shortening the text at the bottom to hit the end time. Another possibility (and trickier) is that you can leave out something in the middle. Some scripts (especially in News) may have optional information in brackets or 'video' (highlighting a phrase or sentence on the computer) that can be left out.

EXERCISE

Look at the following text:

'A study of the future of the English language has predicted that three billion people - nearly half the world's population - will be speaking English by 2015. The study by the British Council (the agency that promotes British culture around the world), suggested that English-language schools could become a

```
victim of their own success and run out of
pupils to teach in fifty years. But the report
argues the popularity of English is unlikely to
threaten other languages. Its author David
Graddol predicts the numbers of Chinese, Arabic
and Spanish speakers are also likely to grow.'
```

This is approximately 38 seconds long. Using a clock or watch with a second-hand which you can easily see next to the text, read it to make it fit a 40-second slot. You can slow up in the last sentence to cruise to the exact 40-second mark. Now try fitting it into a 30-second slot by leaving out the last sentence, coming out on the word 'languages'.

It is important you practise so that you can take your eye off the text – usually between sentences or where there is a break – typically in this script after the word 'years' in line 6, to glance at the clock to see how you are doing. You should be at about 24" at that point.

Finally you could try a 20" version by leaving out the phrase in brackets and coming out on 'years'.

Back-timing

If you want to be very sure of your timing then you can mark with a pencil what the clock should show at a certain point. In the case of the text above for instance – 24" at the word 'years'. If it shows much less than that you will need to slow down to be able to hit the 30" or 40" mark; if it shows more you will need to speed up.

Back-timing is more important in a much longer piece or series of texts where you are fitting a whole programme slot of say 15, 30 or 60 minutes. On radio you will have more responsibility and power over how to fit text into the overall programme time. In TV this will usually be controlled by others.

If you are a continuity announcer then you will need to be very practised in talking to time, as most of what you do will need to fit precise slots.

Meaning-laden words – my version
(see Exercise page 80)

West Lancashire district council, has voted to **ban its workers** from taking **cigarette breaks.** Staff will be **given help** to **give up** but **could face the sack** if they **don't comply** with the **new regulations**, which will be brought in **next March.**

SUMMARY

1. The script is necessary for accuracy and timing. Technical staff depend on the information in it.
2. Prepare by pre-reading aloud, checking for any problems.
3. There are techniques for dealing with monotonous or sing-song delivery.
4. Intonation delivers meaning as well as the words. Find the meaning-laden words and phrases.
5. Break down the script and mark it (with caution) to make it easier to read.
6. There are techniques to fit text into precise time-slots.

7 Ad-libbing

Ad-libbing is extemporising, speaking freely without a script. It might even turn into 'winging it' or even 'flying by the seat of your pants'. It rather depends on whether you expected to be extemporising or not. Then there is the issue of whether that which sounds ad-libbed but is very carefully prepared or semi-scripted is really ad-libbing. I shall deal with these issues as we go along. It would seem in general that we can say ad-libbing is speaking without (or partially without) the benefit of a script.

Some broadcasters might not see a script as a benefit as they are only happy ad-libbing. They do not want to, or cannot work with a script. Music presenters and deejays generally work without a script, although they may refer to notes when giving a line up or particular information that cannot be retained and need not be learned. Reporters at the scene may describe without a script what is going on especially if they are short of time and are live.

Much presentation although keeping to a tight format and timed will be 'off the script', even if certain necessities are acknowledged such as cueing audio or video. Whatever those necessities are, let us look at the techniques behind successful ad-libbing.

PREPARATION

Hearing it and doing it

Some seem effortlessly to be able to talk off the top of their heads and make sense, others panic and clam up in the face of having to speak without aid. And yet surely it is only a question of knowing what you want to say and saying it? Some people are more eloquent than others and can find the right or even cleverly constructed phrases to express themselves, whereas others will be leaden and barely able to get the sense out, and certainly without embellishment. And yet with the aid of preparation we can surely level the playing field.

Hearing a good ad-lib gives the audience the sense that it has been done with little or no preparation – that is part of its charm. But such a reaction also encourages a would-be performer to feel humble: it is a gift, being able to do that, the gift of the gab. You cannot learn that. Can you? Why not?

Scripting it

One way is to literally script it. What do you want to say? Write it as you would say it. Something like this… perhaps?

> *'This sounds good – don't want to butt in here really – just enjoy the music – but have to take a break now 'fraid. Time for some words from the people who pay for it… Oh yeah and it's just coming up to 10 minutes to 4 by the way. You're listening to Drive Time Beat… There's some more Goan Trance coming up after the news…'* etc.

Looking at it one wonders whether it was worth scripting. There is hardly any information (except the time which you can get by simply looking at the clock). It is just chat. It does not fit a slot so there is no timing issue. Try it and see if you can script chat. Obviously you can record chat then transcribe it. But can you say it again exactly as you did the first time, or make it sound as if you are not reading it?

If you can then perhaps it will be useful to script your ad-libs although you will find it cumbersome and time-consuming when you could just be saying it. Looking at the script above: perhaps you should just try saying something similar and see what emerges. Like most things in presentation it will become easier the more you do it. And eventually you will find what works for you.

What is often useful if you have to sound like you are ad-libbing, is to script it, and then give yourself permission to come off the script but always having the security of the script being in front of you. You can also develop a way of partly reading and partly telling the material in your own words. You will need to practise this to find out what suits you.

This is useful for 'interviews' between journalists, where a presenter interviews what is called a 'presenter's friend'; it is also sometimes called a 'starburst' where a journalist responds to a presenter's question on a topic. There may be room for more than one question but the feeling is that the 'visiting' journalist is responding to an interrogative by the presenter. They sound like they are having a conversation but it is a scripted interview where the interviewee responds to pre-arranged questions. However it sounds all the better if the visiting journalist comes off the script somewhat to further the impression of a conversation. If you are on camera without autocue then you will have to be off the script, although you can work from notes. See the paragraph on semi-scripting below.

EXERCISE

Take a 30-second script of any news or feature material. Try coming off the script but sticking closely to what is on the page and see how easily you can make it sound like an ad-lib. It is sometimes useful to two-way it by asking a colleague or friend to ask you questions around the script (you can agree on the questions beforehand), and try to get all the information that is contained in the script in your answers. Record it to check how well you managed it.

This exercise can be useful for those who will be interviewed and who want to keep their answers to a limited amount of information. See Chapter 9 on being interviewed.

Semi-scripting it

More usual is some form of semi-scripting where you work from notes, bullet points or have some material in front of you to refer to, but are largely ad-libbing. This is worth working on because it is a useful skill to be able to work off script like this. It is useful where there are figures or details that cannot be retained without referring to notes.

This form is also helpful when you have to be sure of getting over certain points within a specific time slot. Also it will remind you that you must get things in the right order – that there is a logic and a development and if you miss something out it will make no sense to go back. It is like telling a joke and getting the facts in the wrong order. It doesn't work. Not that you need to tell jokes from notes but you do need to think about their logic.

EXERCISE

Try your hand at being a radio deejay. As the song fades create a link which must contain the following information and in the right order:

- Track: 'It's all over now.'
- A cover of the Rolling Stones song by the Swinging Bilberries.
- Jerry Brown was on lead – Stones fan from young.
- Alex Smith on rhythm.
- Gareth Hill on bass.
- Harry Carter on drums. Liverpudlian – met John Lennon in NY 1979.
- Originally recorded by the Stones in 1964 in Chicago.
- Forthcoming European tour.
- Hammersmith Palais November.
- There used to be over 1000 cover Stones artists. Now there are 35.

- Email from Brian Green says he thinks cover better than the real thing. They're too old now. Who wants to see 70-year-olds dancing around?
- What do you think?
- Email ali@greatsounds.com or phone 020123 4567.
- Next: Van Morrison Astral Weeks album title song.
- Recorded 1968. Only session musicians apart from VM.

Does it sound like you're talking off the top of your head to your audience? Did you manage to turn it into conversation? You can record it and listen back to check.

EXERCISE

Here's another example, this time from the Business News. You need to join up the information into an impromptu script:

- FTSE 6234
- Dow Jones 13 415
- NASDAQ 2596
- Nikkei 16127
- CAC 40 (CAC Quarante) 5565 (Paris Bourse directory)
- Unsteady markets – continuing uncertainty about interbank rates.
- Bank of England helps out Northern Rock Building Soc.
- Chancellor (Darling) – no cause for panic.
- Customers moving money from N. Rock to safer havens.
- Announcement from ECB (Frankfurt) next week and Fed on Thursday.

Note: Numbers can be tricky, especially business indices such as these. It may be better to write the numbers: e.g. 'the Footsie is at six thousand two hundred and thirty four'. Sometimes indices are presented in the following way: 'the Footsie is at sixty two-thirty four.' You should familiarise yourself with common practice if you are doing business news.

Find out what works for you: remember practice makes perfect. In the process of finding your own method and comfort zone you may want to record yourself using a varied array of scripted material. Get to know your own strengths and weaknesses. As with listening to playback, be constructively critical. Change what you can and leave what you cannot. Acknowledge what you do best and what you cannot do. In some cases this is best with the help of a voice or presentation trainer who will be impartial and hopefully help and facilitate a strengthening of your skills.

Being informed

I have worked with extremely talented and knowledgeable journalists who find it easy to talk fluently and logically about a subject (often difficult and involved political stories), as informed commentators, off the script, without notes even. They are extremely good ad-libbers, because they know what they are talking about. There is no replacement for being knowledgeable about what you are going to ad-lib about. Preparation should therefore contain research into the subject you are talking about to make sure you have as much information as you will need – indeed usually more than you will need.

MUSIC PRESENTING

Presenting music programmes is a specialist field. Some presenters or deejays are personalities and will have developed an on-air identity which is individual and established so the listeners tune in as much for the deejays as the music. Some presenters offer specialist music (classical, popular or particular) and attract an audience who have specifically tuned in for the music. The presenter is there for information. There may be a mix of current affairs, news, chat and music as is often the case in local radio and at breakfast and drive-time.

Focussing on what you need to get across will probably be your best ally in linking music tracks. You will need notes to work from.

Talking up to the vocals

Techniques such as talking up to the vocals on music tracks although something to be mastered, must be a style decision. It can sound hackneyed if used too smoothly and frequently. It involves timing and rehearsing so that you can fit what you say to exactly the precise slot. Talking up to the vocals involves timing the instrumental introduction to a track to the point where the vocals start and talking up to that point. You will start the music according to how much you have to say in order to fit the speech exactly to the time allowed before the vocals. You may well have kept the musical intro faded down under your speech and then bring the music up (on the fader) for the vocals.

Interaction

Interacting with the audience in any way, whether reading out their requests or talking on the phone, involves a certain tone. You need to show that you are pleased to play requests and that you do not take your audience for granted. You will be judged by that tone, and you will have to think carefully about the relationship you want to create with the audience.

Remember – always keep it simple. Do not try to get too much over in one link. Keep your audience with you, allow them to digest the information. Do not get ahead of yourself. It will become easier, more natural the more you do it.

PIECES TO CAMERA

You are on location – outside broadcast – so no autocue. Not much time to prepare and you need to do a PTC (piece to camera). You do not have time to write a piece of 30 or 40 seconds and memorise it, and in any case it will probably be better for not being memorised. You will have to ad-lib but that does not mean you do not prepare. You can write notes. You could start with a sentence that sums up what you want to say. You could expand on this by writing down a few bullet points. And you could think about the person whom you want to tell this to.

EXERCISE

Take a situation, any situation – look out of the window and find one. Sum it up in a sentence. For example:

> ***'The main road outside my home is always busy with waste management trucks, so they should relocate the waste headquarters to a quieter location out of town.'***

Now expand it into several (three or four) points:

1. Constant traffic day and night.
2. Waste dumper trucks from all over London.
3. Location of Waste HQ.
4. Advantage of changing location.

Now practise your piece to fill about 30 or 40 seconds. This will be a report on the situation you have chosen. Stand and deliver it to camera. If you have video, record it. If not, no matter, you will know how well you do.

The expertise to make this good will necessarily come with practice, so try it several times. This is the sort of exercise you can do while you are out and about (without the video recording though). If for instance you are travelling look out of the car, bus or train window. Here are a few tips:

- Focus your mind on telling the story. What are you trying to get over? Think logically.
- Think about whom you are telling this to. If it helps, visualise a particular person.
- You need to focus your mind so as not to allow anything to distract you, which is why it helps to practise outside with people around. There will be plenty of distractions for your real PTC.
- Take a moment to relax in front of the camera (imaginary or real). It sometimes works better if you do not start in the moment you are cued (or cue yourself). Take your time.

- Think about the emotion of the piece if it has any and get that across to your audience.
- Be clear and economical in your style. No waffle or unnecessary content.
- Check yourself against these standards. Watch reporters perform on TV and pick up tips from them.

DEALING WITH THE UNEXPECTED

Sometimes ad-libs are called for to deal with the unexpected. If you are live and something goes wrong, you may be called on to ad-lib: for instance if there are technical problems with the equipment, lines go down, there are unexpected gaps or mistakes in the script, the autocue jams, last-minute developments, difficult interviewees. There are many forms of the unexpected. How can you deal with such things in a calm way?

Staying calm

If you are behind the mic or camera when something goes wrong, that is where you are going to stay for the moment before a decision is made about what to do in a situation such as any of the above. Acknowledging that and being honest with your audience is all you can do. In fact you should often take the audience into your confidence unless it would be particularly counter-productive to do so. They know you are live (or should do), and so also know that the unexpected can happen. Telling them what is going on (as you see it) should be a natural reaction to the unexpected. This will have the effect of calming you, as you engage your audience in this way.

I used almost to enjoy things going wrong in the radio news studio when I was behind the mic. While the problem was being sorted out by frantic producers and technical staff, I could do nothing other than engage with my audience. That was my job. The mistake and subsequent ad-lib reminded the audience that it was a live programme and we could but wait till things were fixed (if it was a technical hitch). Of course I needed standby material to fill with, which I had, so I could only engage them with that until I was given further instructions from those who were producing the programme.

I knew a radio newsreader who realised too late that he did not have his spectacles with him prior to reading the news to at least 40 million listeners around the world. As he opened the fader (to activate the mic) on the hour, all he could say after identifying himself, the station and a time check, was to apologise for not being able to read the news as he didn't have his glasses with him. There was some frantic activity in the newsroom as his specs were found. He remained calm and did the only thing he could do – be honest.

A word about apologies. Remember they underline mistakes. They remind the audience, who may not have realised, that a mistake has been made. But they are often necessary to dispel any possible confusion in the audience's mind. And as I say above it establishes an honest relationship with your audience if you can share the problem with them. Be careful not to blame anyone on air for mistakes – producers or technicians, for instance. They will not be amused!

FILLING TO TIME

There are several possible situations in which you may have to fill to time. One frequent one is at the end of a programme, since that is often where the presenter will either have to soak up extra time or be brief to fill the slot available. You will have to think about what you will need if there is more time available than expected.

Filling possibilities

It is often the case that the presenter has to fill up to 30 seconds but it could be up to three or four minutes and I have known longer. It depends on the programme, the station and the stand-by material available. On a professional radio network the continuity announcer may fill to time as part of their schedule – and as part of their job. Likewise a news presenter may fill to time at the end of a programme if the programme does not have a signature tune to fill to the end time (pre-fade). These are not situations where something unexpected has happened – it is merely filling to the slot.

If the programme has had an under-run on a live interview for instance and there has not been enough time to play a whole other item then the presenter may find him or herself with a substantial gap. It is therefore necessary to think about this possibility beforehand and have material ready.

Here are some possibilities:

Idents

Idents identify the station, network or programme.

Example

Station idents are popular. For example:

> *'You're listening to Radio Star on 104.4, digital, satellite and on the web – radiostar.com. News, weather, business – around the clock.'*

That takes 10 seconds to say, give or take a second or two. If your time slot is 7 seconds you can shorten it to fit. For example:

> *'You're listening to Radio Star on 104.4, digital, satellite and on the web – radio star.com.'*

If it is 14 seconds you will need more:

> *'You're listening to Radio Star broadcasting on 104.4, digital, satellite and on the web – www.radiostar.com. All you need in news, business and weather reports – 24 hours a day.'*

There are name and time checks:

> *'I'm Alec Sabin and it's coming up to 24 minutes past 8 (you're listening to Breakfast here on Radio Star).'*

That was 4 seconds without the programme and station ident; 8 seconds with them.

Experiment with your own ideas and try to fill different pre-arranged slots of between 5 and 30 seconds.

Interactivity

There is also the possibility of interactive prompts: the website, the email address, the phone numbers. You can read out emails that listeners have sent in. They are not only good filler material but are also important to keep the emails coming. If you want response, which most radio and TV stations do to confirm interest in their programming, then you need to read out correspondence so the audience know you are serious about wanting their input. It stimulates interest and debate. You will be ad-libbing around these items, of course.

More information

Then there is the weather or, if it is a news or current affairs programme, you could go back to the top story, or the headlines once again. These are not ad-libbed of course but they can be fitted into a wider fill. To know what is most appropriate is to know the programme, so the choice will be up to you who will make it work because you are in control.

From ad-lib to script

One skill that the above throws up is the ability to move from ad-libbing to scripted material (and vice versa) without an obvious change of delivery style. If you are ad-libbing into a cue to a recorded item, for example, the audience should not be aware of where the ad-lib ends and the scripted material starts. You might précis an email if pushed for time by editing it. For example:

'John doesn't agree with the last correspondent – he says that "we should cut our carbon emissions straight away without waiting for other countries".'

This will of course be only part of John's email.

CONTINUITY

Broadcasting is ruled by the clock: programme times are precise. Continuity announcers along with network directors on TV, who look after the transmission of the programmes as per the schedule, produce the links, promotional material, and putting the programmes, whether pre-recorded or live, to air. Continuity announcers need to be able to fill to time exactly. Usually the material is prepared and often scripted, but they must be able to ad-lib to time too. Knowing what material is suitable usually comes with experience and the longer you have been with a particular station or network the more easily it comes off the tongue. But bear in mind the following adage posted up in a continuity studio I worked in:

'Just when you thought the presentation was going well so'.

It doesn't always come out quite how you intended, however confident and experienced you are.

The worth of a presentation or continuity department lies in the seamless presentation of programmes that delivers a channel or station/network: that helps the audience identify it and that in turn will encourage them to come back for more. In their function to not only link but also promote programmes, continuity announcers serve the network. I mention this only to underline that what you are doing should be contained in the motivation for any ad-libs. Knowing that that is what you must do should colour your ad-libs, since you must not only be a professional speaker to time and technician (you will often have to operate the equipment), but also a salesperson. And that function will call on your personal qualities to attract and keep the audience with you.

Most radio stations will not have continuity announcers; the presenters will not only have their own programmes but also be required to link to others and promote them, as well as self-operating the studio and also, if the station is commercial, playing advertising material.

SUMMARY

1. The best ad-libs are often the best-prepared ones.
2. Find your own strengths by scripting or semi-scripting them.
3. Music presenting may be about personality or information.
4. Pieces to camera can be perfected. Focus is important.
5. Share problems of the unexpected with your audience if appropriate. It will help to keep you calm.
6. There are standard stand-bys for filling to time. It is best to practise and be prepared.
7. Continuity announcers need to fill to time, link programmes, operate the equipment and sell and promote the station/network – sometimes all at the same time.

Interviewing 8

What is an interview?

An interview is a dialogue. As far back as the Ancient Greek philosophers, information and ideas have been presented in question-and-answer form. The tradition is pedagogic. It pertains to teaching and the philosophical tradition of the dialectic where an idea creates a challenge which is then resolved through dialogue. It may seem artificial and indeed it is an artifice (as an interview is), but it is an attractive and convincing form of disseminating ideas. The form offers the reader, listener or viewer something more than a monologue which could be interpreted as unopposed presentation of material, even a rant or diatribe. In dialogue form the information must be modified to satisfy an interlocutor who acts on our behalf. It therefore has more authority.

Interviewing is a skill that when done well (like so many things) sounds easy: in fact hardly like an interview at all – more like a conversation. In some ways it is a conversation, in others it certainly is not. It is conversation in that it is talk between two people, but it is structured, often strictly timed, prepared for and designed to extract information; it is more a device than a free-wheeling conversation. The form of the interview will be dominated by the reason for it. Are you trying to extract something from a wily politician, get the low down from a celebrity or perhaps information from an expert? Knowing what you want will determine how you get it.

WHY INTERVIEW?

It is as well to ask yourselves why conduct an interview when you could just as easily give your audience the information that you have hitherto gleaned from the interviewee off-mic or camera. But apart from that being a rather boring way to present information the audience needs to see the interviewee giving the information. Why? There are three main reasons. Impartiality – you cannot tamper with the information; authority – it is from the horse's mouth; entertainment and immediacy – the audience does not want to hear about the interviewee, they want to see or hear him or her for themselves.

Unpredictability

There is also an unpredictable quality about any interview even if it is recorded and edited. The interviewee is free to answer your well prepared questions in any way they so choose, which may reveal something that was unlooked-for but necessary or interesting nevertheless. It is this unexpected (and uncontrollable) quality that often gives the interview its essential appeal.

Preparation

Decide why you want the interview and what you want out if it. This may seem like stating the obvious but with time often being a constraint it is as well to ask yourself these simple questions in order to get the best from your interviewee. Interviews are often plagued by long questions or waffle where lack of a clear purpose is the fault. Lack of preparation dogs a potentially good interview. How often have you thought that the interviewer is not asking the right question, letting the politician off the hook, or leaving the celebrity in obscurity?

Do your research so that you will know what to ask in the time available. Sometimes lack of preparation is unavoidable. I once found myself unexpectedly standing next to Princess Stephanie of Monaco, with a broadcast recorder over my shoulder. I asked her for the interview and she consented. But then as I knew so little of her recent life my questions were open and vague. She helped me on her recent forays into the pop-music business, but not much on her personal life. It is notoriously difficult to get interviews with some celebrities, so it was disappointing that I did not have much of real interest to listen to when I played it back for broadcast.

ASKING THE RIGHT QUESTIONS

Doing your preparation and knowing what you want will direct you to asking the right questions. There are no hard and fast rules governing the right questions since interviews are organic – more biochemistry than mathematics. However it is as well to bear in mind that if you ask questions that prompt a yes/no answer then that is what you may get, which will be insufficient if, as you usually do, you want a fuller response. Questions starting with the words 'is, are, do, did, have, had, will, would, should, could, might, can' allow for a simple yes/no answer. It depends on your interviewee.

'Have you always wanted to be a musician?' may well prompt a simple *'Yes'*, leaving you to ask the next question. The respondent may follow it up themselves. *'Ever since I can remember – I remember tinkling on the piano when I was three…'* etc.

If you are confident you have a loquacious speaker then there is less risk of one-word answers to these questions and if you have a follow up ready (*'what is your earliest memory of music?'*), then all will be fine.

If you just need a yes/no to an important question: *'are you going to resign?'* that is obviously fine. But a better question might be: *'when are you going to resign?'* or *'why are you not going to resign?'* where the question is more provocative and moves the interview forward faster.

Be careful not to ask two questions together since the interviewee may either not know which one to answer, forget to answer one of them, or choose the one they want to answer.

Get to the point

In order to get straightforward information you only have to ask for it. I am amazed how some people find this difficult to do. The English sometimes are not direct, thinking it impolite. They like to warm up before asking direct questions. This is not appropriate in an interview since you do not have time for niceties. That is not to say you should be rude but you need to state clearly from the start what you want. If there are difficult or sensitive areas in an interview it is certainly good practice not to start with them, and you can warm up your respondent with less controversial questions to start. But you are still interviewing and time is always at a premium. Make your introductory questions relevant to the subject at hand.

Starting the interview

Do not use preamble in the interview: do it beforehand if it is necessary at all. Short courtesies are in order, especially if the interviewee is on the phone, such as *'good morning, Mr Smith'* (having introduced him as John Smith in the cue). You need to check he is there, and that he can hear you, resolved by his response – (*'good morning'*), then you can get straight into your first question. Do not go in for too much *'thank you for coming on the programme'*, and *'I wonder if I might ask you...'* This is superfluous. A proper introduction is necessary and all you need by way of preamble.

What, where, who, when, why, how?

All of these prompt fuller answers and 'why' and 'how' questions are particularly useful to elicit longer and revealing answers. They can also act as supplementary questions. If you feel an answer does not fully answer the question or the respondent has more information that they have not revealed, 'how' and 'why' can act as good probing cues.

For example:

1. *'What are the main features of this new invention?'*
   (Answer): *Speed, it is green-friendly, and it's cheap.*
   'How is it green-friendly?'

2. *'You're a Samaritan. Tell us about that.'*
   (Answer): *Well I wanted to give something back to society.*
   'Why?'

'Tell us' can be used to get your respondent to talk. If they are responding well then you will need more specific questions to steer the interview where you want it: *'How exactly does this follow from what you have just told us?' 'Why are you announcing this now?'*

The pre-interview discussion

Important information can be gleaned from a pre-interview discussion with the interviewee which is essential. This is where you may find out areas that you have not thought of, so you may want to change your questions having learned something new at this stage. It will also relax a nervous interviewee since you can give the impression that you have already started the interview – just not turned the mic or camera on. You will also need to tell your interviewee how long you want, what the interview is for, how it will be edited and what areas you want to cover. Do not, however, rehearse the interview, and do not tell the interviewee your questions beforehand, except the first one. You need the answers to be spontaneous.

TYPES OF INTERVIEW

There are different kinds of interview with different functions:

- factual
- expert
- investigative
- entertainment

are among the most often used in the media.

The factual interview

The factual interview exists to transmit information. Uncontentious as this may seem, the very presentation of information can give rise to controversy: there may be different versions of an event seen from the points of view of two eyewitnesses. The factual interview does not deny that the information can be disputed. It is an account of the facts. The interviewee must therefore be identified since the audience will then know whose account it is.

Getting the information

Straightforward information-gathering can be obtained by using the what, where, who and when interrogatives. Eyewitnesses can be encouraged to give facts quite simply, with little prompting:

- *'What happened when the tornado struck your house?'*
- *'Where were you?'*
- *'Who was with you?'* etc.

The story will unfold. 'Why' and 'how' questions may prompt more thought and judgement:

- *'Why didn't you leave the house?'*
  (Answer): *Because my baby was asleep upstairs and I didn't want to leave him.*
- *'How did you rescue your baby?'*
  (Answer): *I managed to climb on to the balcony and get in to the bedroom after smashing the window.*

The questions you ask presuppose the answers you want. But that does not mean you know what the answer will be. You ask *'what happened then?'* knowing that the interviewee will cover the part of the story when and just after the tornado hit the house: that is what you want. You do not know exactly that the answer will be:

> *There was an almighty crash, and blinding light, the roof split down the middle – I could see the sky – the next thing I knew was that furniture from my upstairs bedroom was now in the downstairs living room.*

While it is true as a general rule that you should not ask questions prompting a yes/no answer you may want to ask:

> *'Wasn't it dangerous to climb into the bedroom after the roof had fallen in?'* prompting the answer *It may well have been but I wanted to save my baby.*

Knowing what you want, having done the research and perhaps having had an opportunity to talk to your interviewee before recording or broadcasting the interview (if live), will direct your questions. And so if you do not get what you want you may persist. If the answer to the last question was: *I don't know, I just did it*, you may follow with:

> *'Why didn't you wait for the fire brigade?'* looking for *I just wanted to save my baby.*

The expert interview

You go to experts for information, but also analysis. Medical, legal and academic respondents can give information within their fields with authority. However, care needs to be taken. Such experts can be opinionated and biased. You may need to balance their contributions with those of others (equally expert, of course).

In addition they may have difficulty explaining their expertise to the lay public. You may need to get them to clarify or simplify in everyday language. Also make sure they know that they only have a limited time to get their point across. And you will need to take control over how much analysis you want, and on which point:

- *'Does this new drug cure all forms of the disease?'*
  Answer: *Well, new forms are emerging all the time but it is certainly a step forward from what is on offer at the moment.*
- *'How does it differ from previous drugs?'*
  Answer: *Well, the science is different...*
- *'So in layman's terms it strengthens the immune system?'*
  Answer: *You could see it like this...*
- *'Do you think developing countries in Africa can look forward to decreasing mortality?'*
  Answer: *That's a big question – it rather depends on the drug company's policy on pricing...*

Expert interviews need to be tightly controlled and the more preparation you do the better. You can tell your respondent exactly what you want and, perhaps more importantly, what you do not want. Referring to the typical audience member and time constraints will provide you with reasons for your demands. However you also need to know roughly what the answers are before you ask the questions so you can get to the essential information and avoid what you do not want, or do not have time for.

The investigative interview

At the sharper end of journalistic enquiry – in hard news for instance – the interviewer investigates, and, perhaps like the detective, is dealing with a not necessarily co-operative interviewee. But the principle of knowing what you want beforehand (which applies to other forms of interview) still pertains. With investigation you may have to pursue and persevere. Your interviewee may well not be obstructive but neither will s/he be helpful. You need to be focussed so that if you think s/he is evasive then you must repeat the question or put it another way to get what you want. There are also cultural considerations: in some countries it is not customary to harass politicians or other important personnel (as it is in the UK), but equally with the rise of spin and public relations initiatives, these interviewees know how to protect themselves in whatever culture.

Research

If you have done your research and are therefore aware of differing opinions for instance, you can use them to challenge your interviewee. It is advisable to attribute opposing opinions to emphasise that they are not held by you. Indeed it is important that you are seen by the audience and respondent alike, to maintain an impartial view in order to expose evasion, and put your interviewee on the spot. If they can dismiss you as partial, or if you are in any way impolite or aggressive in your questioning rather than assertive and persistent, then an experienced interviewee will turn things to their own advantage and gain the support of the audience in the process:

> *'The opposition says (would say) that your economic forecast is optimistic – because of public spending last year you are going to have to find economies in the coming financial year, how are you going to do that?'*

is better than:

> *'Everyone knows that you overspent last year and you are in this mess now because of incompetence.'*

Having said that there are well-known current affairs interviewers who might prefer the latter approach since it provokes and shows the interviewee that they are not going to get away with regurgitating press-release material. But only one or two can get away with it, and perhaps that style should be left to those that have made it their own.

The experienced interviewee

Politicians and others who have probably had the benefit of media training may try to use the interview as a platform to advertise a particular point of view or make a statement. They not only do not answer your questions but instead answer their own. They come with prepared answers, whatever your questions, and try to hijack the interview for their own purposes. This will necessitate the interviewer taking back control. You can politely remind the interviewee that they have not answered the question and/or repeat it. Keep to your pre-arranged line. Try not to be deflected. You can interrupt which will be forgiven if there is good reason for it. Do not get argumentative – remain calm and stand your ground. If you become aggressive or personal you will lose the support of the audience and will not get what you want from the interviewee either.

Dodgy ones

What applies to a politician may not be suitable for someone you think needs to be exposed. Nevertheless, however persistent you are with your questioning, be careful of the libel laws and make sure you have interviews 'legalled' (i.e.

checked) by experts if you are in any doubt, and know what defences there are available. You cannot call someone corrupt, but you can ask them if they paid someone, or received a sum of money. This kind of journalism is a speciality which requires expertise and plenty of preparation.

The entertainment interview

This is a wide bracket containing not only celebrity interviews but what may be termed feature interviews where someone is asked about their interest, occupation or expertise, and which can also stray into the factual and expert categories above. However if the subject of the interview has entertainment value, and here we can include sports men and women, then it is not only the facts that interest us but who is telling them. The focus shifts to the interviewee themselves: how they feel, how they express themselves, as much as what they say. In fact in the age of reality TV, the interviewee may have little actual information to impart and are not known to us outside the programme, but the media have elevated them to a level of interest in the audience's mind in spite of this, which make them viable entertainment interviewees.

Having done your research for the interview you must allow the interviewee to entertain. They may have prepared anecdotes and interesting illustrative stories which you can elicit with the right questions. Remember you are still working within a time schedule and need to be aware of how much you can get through. In order to get what you want you may have to use your personality to encourage and cajole.

Certain celebs (and musicians in particular) may not be as articulate as others, and so you will have to work harder at getting them to express themselves. The focus may move to your powers to be an interested conversationalist as such interviews seem to emulate chat, but the purpose should not be far from your mind. And although you are giving the impression that you are enjoying yourself (which you are if you are engaging the interviewee and the audience) you always have an agenda and you need to keep to it.

Guests on live daytime TV and radio shows are often there to promote something – a book, play, film, programme or event. They may be there as part of a PR campaign. The more information you have the better such an interview will be. If you have read the book or seen the play or film then your input will make the interview more interesting:

> *'Tell us about your new book/play/film. Is it a departure from your usual area of interest?'*

does not work as well as:

> *'This one is a departure from your usual area of interest. It's darker and funnier. Some might even think with a particular moral angle. Are you exploring new ground here?'*

If you are interviewing live between music tracks, make sure each section has substance. You may need to recap after a track to remind listeners and tell new joiners what has gone before and importantly whom you are interviewing. Discipline in keeping control of the time and getting plenty of information from your guest with the right questions will pay off.

If there are two presenters as is customary in some of these kinds of shows, make sure you know what your co-presenter is going to do. There will be a form of script on TV and perhaps some use of auto-cue. On radio either you will take it in turns to interview in which case there is no problem, or one of you will be the lead interviewer with an occasional supplementary question allowed from the co-presenter. The chemistry between presenters is another issue. That will need to be developed separately.

WHAT IS THE INTERVIEW FOR?

Interviews may appear in their entirety, as they are when broadcast live, but often they are edited to form part of a larger whole. How ever they will finally appear (and what part of them) the interviewer needs to be aware of that final form, as it will inevitably influence how the interview is managed. If, for instance, you just want a 20-second sound-bite, there is no point in carrying out an in-depth 20-minute interview. You can stop recording as soon as you get what you want. Many edited forms will remove the questions, and feature only parts of the interviewee's answers.

It is also important to tell your interviewee what the interview will be used for, that it will be edited and how it will be broadcast.

Here are some formats:

- A package (or short mini-feature) with several extracts from different interviews.
- A documentary with edited extracts from a range of interviewees representing differing fields of expertise, viewpoints and opinions.
- A live discussion in the studio with interviewees representing differing or opposing views.
- An interview to be broadcast either live or recorded before or after another differently opinionated one, or commentary by a reporter, or discussion, or following or preceding a package or feature.
- A vox pop. Differing reactions from the general public to the same question edited together.
- The phone interview and phone-ins.

The package

A radio package is a form which features extracts from interviews, actuality or sounds that set a scene, music perhaps, and sometimes other pre-recorded material from other reports. It is edited usually by the reporter who is commissioned with telling the story through creative use of the material. It is typically four or five minutes, with a cue (read by the studio presenter) introducing the topic and giving some introductory information but also providing a link into the opening part of the package which may be actuality, the voice of the reporter/interviewer or the first extract of an interview. The form usually includes at least two or three extracts from at least two interviewees but may just be two extracts from the same interview. The extracts illustrate a logical form whereby the reporter tells the story. A simple example from News would be:

Example

Cue (read by studio presenter, live) explaining the latest developments of a strike, and name of reporter:

Package

1. sounds from the picket line;
2. reporter telling us about the strike and introducing shop steward;
3. shop steward explaining grievance (extract from interview);
4. link by reporter with more information and introducing management spokesperson;
5. management explaining their position (extract from interview);
6. concluding wrap by reporter.

In conducting interviews for packages you need to know what you want. You will have chosen interviewees to represent certain standpoints (although they may surprise you with what they say, so there is always the possibility that the package will change because of what an interviewee comes out with). If you are after 20, 30 or 40 seconds from your interviewee giving information or expressing a certain opinion make sure that that is what you get. You can do this by asking the right question to elicit it and allowing them to say it without interruption. You also should tell your interviewee what the final form will be.

Your questions will mostly be edited out of the final cut; nevertheless the links that you will write and present need to fit with what you have your interviewee saying in the package. If you have your shop steward saying: *'we're all out and we're staying out till we get what we want'* your lead into that could be: *'shop steward Bert Smith on the picket line with colleagues was in no mood for compromise.'*

Also notice that your linking material leading into your clips can set them up, as I do above, without giving away what your interviewee is going to say. So not *'I spoke to Bert Smith who told me they were staying out on strike'* which makes for a bad segue (or link between two sources, in this case the presenter's lead-in and the clip of Bert Smith), since it would be followed by *'...we're all out and we're staying out till we get what we want'.* Rather what I suggest in the previous paragraph would be better.

The documentary

The documentary allows more scope than the package because it is longer and generally explores a subject in more depth. There are more extracts with several from a single interview possible. While a radio package can be conceived, researched, written, presented and edited by one person (who also does the interviewing), a documentary is more often a team effort. Only in radio could it also be a one-person production – but it is more probably subject to others' contributions. For that reason the interviewing involved will be subject to discussion before and after the interviews.

For example when I made 30-minute radio documentaries, arranging, conducting and editing all the interviews, collecting all the music and recording sounds (known as wild track) needed for the final edit, when I came to record my presentation and put it all together, I was joined by a studio technician and a producer who made last-minute editorial changes.

You will need to have an outline of the end product in your mind before you do the interviews. This will focus your area of questioning. It will give you an agenda to get through. The responses by the interviewees will be edited and scattered throughout the programme, with questions edited out. You may be covering the same ground with different interviewees, or looking for a different opinion on a topic.

With both packages and documentaries the programme is as good as the contributions from the interviewees. If you have got some good stuff from your interviewees then they will carry the programme. You will just need to package it. It is therefore up to you to get that material to produce a quality programme.

A live discussion

If you have more than one guest in a discussion on a topic you will need to manage their contributions. They may have opposing viewpoints which makes your job similar to that of the chair in a debate, where you make sure all the guests are given a fair hearing. They can be encouraged to ask and answer questions themselves but you are there to keep (or take) control. More often the guests will represent different but not necessarily opposing positions, and then your job is to make sure all those views with attendant information are aired.

You need to prepare by knowing what each guest's position and area of expertise is so you can prompt their contributions with the right questions. And you need to know which respondent is the best person to answer which question. The job requires a range of skills. You need to encourage and cajole, but also to control and interrupt, be courteous yet firm, knowledgeable but interested, impartial, sensitive and have a sense of humour. I am sure there are other qualities that are desirable, but what is important is that the discussion sheds heat and light on a subject and that as presenter you need to try to make sure this happens within the time constraints with everyone getting a fair crack of the whip.

If you are a guest you will need to develop the skills which are outlined in the next chapter. You need to know why you are there and what is expected of you. Your contribution will be affected by what others in the programme are saying which although you may have no prior knowledge of, you can with research and knowing something about your co-guests, get an idea of what they might offer. Such preparation will pay dividends.

What comes before or after the interview?

Some interviews, or parts of them, succeed or precede others on the same topic, probably from a different viewpoint. They may form part of a programme segment which includes a discussion, package or report. Some parts may be recorded, others live. Not only do you as interviewer need to know (sometimes only roughly) what is intended by the producer, but you need to inform your interviewee of it too.

If the interview follows a report, for instance, you can ask for a reaction to it. If your interviewee knows s/he will be followed by someone else on the same topic they may try to counter what they know of their position. You can perhaps warn them that you will be asking the same question of their successor. In general it is as well for both interviewer and interviewee to know where the interview sits in a programme segment and how it will be used.

It is part of your job to give as accurate a description of what the interview is for as possible and how it will be edited. You are also ethically bound not to edit an interview to misrepresent what an interviewee intended.

Vox pops

'Vox populi' means the voice of the people. Editors use vox pops to present a range of opinions from the general public on a single issue. In such interviews the same question is asked of a number of people in a public place and then edited favouring only the responses not the repeated question. They are usually conducted outside, in the street or public place such as a shopping mall, and give the impression that they are a random sample of Joe Public on a particular issue – a snapshot of public opinion. Editors like them because they are relatively easy to do and are interesting and seemingly valid without having to do a great deal of research. They are not representative, of course, since the sampling is not controlled and the editor decides how wide a range of opinions are finally broadcast.

If opinion is canvassed about an issue that is the domain of a certain group of people then the interviews should take place where there are plenty of those people. For example if the question is to be *'what do you think of the provision for cyclists on the road in the city?'* then you will need to find a place where there are plenty of cyclists but also motorists and pedestrians since their opinions will be useful and relevant on such an issue. You may have to find them in different locations: a cycle park, a station forecourt and on a busy pavement, for example.

What is important is that their answers are in response to the same question. You can ask supplementary questions to probe further:

Question:	*'What do you think of the provision for cyclists on the road in the city?'*
Answer:	*'I think it is inadequate.'*
Probe:	*'Why?'*
Answer:	*'There aren't enough cycle lanes. Especially in the centre...'*

The editor will sometimes cut out your questions, although keeping them in shows that the exercise was fair (such editing is easier in audio than video). However it is the responses and not the repeated questions that are important for the finished product.

Your job is to try to get as many people as possible to respond in order to get a good sample – not always easy since many people avoid such interviews in the street. You must also ask the same question even when you may be tempted to put it another way. *'What's wrong with cyclists in the city?' 'Should drivers be persuaded out of their cars and on to bikes?'* may get things going but you cannot ask different questions of your respondents and represent them as if they had answered the same question.

The phone-in

Interviewing callers in a phone-in programme can be an exciting process. Like the vox pop there is sometimes a veneer of representative opinion which is illusory since those who phone radio programmes (and TV) are not a representative sample of the public. They are probably people who have phoned in before, they have strong opinions, they may be belligerent, or humorous or they like the sound of their own voices. Sometimes callers can be screened by an assistant before putting them to air; or the station can sometimes phone back callers who have previously phoned to take part.

The role of the presenter is to be fair and, as in the discussion above, manage opinion through different contributors. The unpredictability of the phone-in can make that difficult but it also makes it good listening. The expression of strong feelings makes good radio but you have to watch out for the offensive, libellous or defamatory as well as the boring, unintelligible, inarticulate or irrelevant. Because you are dealing with the public rather than chosen 'representatives' different skills are needed. Some phone-in presenters are encouraged to provoke and may take an editorially one-sided view to get things going.

The phone-in presenter tends to be a personality presenter like the deejay. Callers often treat him or her as if they know them. Indeed some encourage regular callers especially if they need all they can get. I knew one late-night phone-in presenter tell Doris of Walthamstow (who was a regular), that while she was 'going on' he was going to go to the toilet. And he did, confident that when he got back to the studio Doris would still be talking: she was – '*... and another thing...*'

USEFUL TECHNIQUE

- **Do a pre-interview discussion.** Find out as much as you can, discuss areas of interest.
- **Think about what areas you want to cover.** Just bullet points can work. They are often more flexible than precise questions.

- **If you write your questions down you do not have to keep to them.** You can write down and stick to your first question but after that questions may depend on answers.
- **Do not tell the interviewee the questions except the first one.** You need to keep control and flexibility to change questions.
- **Listen to the answers.** It is very important to listen to your interviewee (and not be thinking of your next question), as you might miss important information. Answers may prompt different or supplementary or repeat questions.
- **Probe and ask supplementary questions.** Get the interviewee to clarify or expand, if too brief or unclear.
- **Do not be argumentative, personal or emotional.** Do not get involved in emotional exchange however provoking the interviewee is. It is counterproductive. Stick with getting what you set out to do. Represent dissent by referring to others not self. 'Some people might say...'
- **Repeat questions if necessary.** Experienced interviewees answer their own questions, if yours are too challenging. Repeat the question to get what you want.
- **Don't ask multiple questions.** Otherwise the interviewee will choose which question to answer or forget one.
- **Tell the interviewee what it is for.** Tell them how it will be edited – whether part of a programme, who else is being interviewed and how long the final product is likely to be.
- **Reassure nervous interviewees.** Explain the technology (especially TV). Pre-discussion can relax interviewees. Try to get them to treat it like a conversation.
- **Don't add ums and ahs – stay silent during the answers.** When you come to edit it will be frustrating if there is noise or a voice other than the interviewee talking. Smile and nod to encourage rather than using verbal prompts.
- **Don't record a lot more than you will need.** It is bad practice (you must control the time if live). But it is unnecessary to record a lot more than needed. Decide beforehand what you want in the time available.

- **Don't add unnecessary preamble.** It distracts from the matter in hand. Introduce, greet and get on with it. At the end say thank you and/or goodbye. You can have a chat after the interview.
- **If the interviewee gives interesting information after you have finished recording, turn the mic/camera back on again.** Sometimes interviewees come out with good stuff after the interview because they are relaxed now they are off-mic or camera. Turn it back on and with their permission record some more.
- **Ask questions the audience want answered.** You are representing the audience, asking the questions they want answered, drawing an interviewee out for their benefit.
- **The interviewee is more important than the interviewer.** The important one is the interviewee and what they have to say, no matter how knowledgeable you are on the topic. Remembering that will get more out of your interviewee and gain the respect of the audience.

SUMMARY

1. Interviews may sound like conversations but are more structured and controlled.
2. Decide what you want and why you want it.
3. Think about the kind of questions that elicit the answers you want.
4. There are different types of interview requiring different interviewing techniques e.g. factual, investigative, entertainment.
5. Investigative interviews with experienced interviewees require special skill. Do your homework.
6. Interviews serve packages, documentaries, vox pops, discussions, phone-ins and other formats. Know what the end product is.
7. Bear in mind some basic principles of interviewing.

Being interviewed 9

Being interviewed can be an unnerving experience especially for those who are new to it. There is often a misconception that the interviewee will be able to control the interview and how it subsequently appears, when that is rarely the reality. Even if the interview is broadcast live interviewees can be surprised when they watch or listen to the playback. If the interviewer is experienced and good at their job they will make the interviewee feel they are in control, relaxed and that all of what they have to say is equally important and interesting. Interviewees may be disappointed if that is not what they feel when they see the playback. Often interviewees feel that they are misrepresented even during a live interview. This chapter is for those, as interviewees, who want to learn some techniques for getting the best out of a broadcast interview.

Being a guest on the media usually involves a variation of the interview. If you are in a studio audience you may have the opportunity of asking the questions yourself, although you may be lucky to ask more than one! But whatever the programme, it is as well to think about the bigger picture of which you as a guest are only a part. Understanding your role will help you perform well.

WHAT YOU NEED TO KNOW BEFORE THE INTERVIEW

In the previous chapter I discussed the differing objectives of interviews. Your behaviour, as interviewee, should be modified according to those objectives. If the interviewer is after a sound-bite – a slogan – then give them one: there is no point in rambling on for 5 minutes if they are after 15 seconds. If they want anecdotes then you should have prepared some and even discussed them with the interviewer prior to the interview. You need to find out what the interview is for and how it is going to be used.

Recorded or live?

If the interview is recorded then it will probably be edited. You need to know what the final format of the programme will be and the duration of your contribution. There is no reason why the interviewer should not tell you before the interview what it is for and how much s/he wants. In fact the interviewer may tell you what s/he wants you to say. You may certainly be asked the same questions several times, and you are free, of course, to stop and go back. But this should always be done with the final format in mind. If they are after a clip or particular information, you can stop and go back if you think you can improve on your answer.

If the interview is live then perforce there will be no editing – no stopping and going back. You can still find out how much they want and what they expect of you. You will not normally be invited to see the questions beforehand (except perhaps the first one). The interviewer may repeat questions or probe. You have less control with live broadcasting, but equally the interviewer has no control over what you are going to say. Live interviews need to be prepared for if you want to get the best out of them. Sometimes, however, they are more satisfying since they are one-off and can produce creative results because they rely on spontaneity. Although interviewers will probably be more experienced than you are at live broadcasting, they will be nervous too. Try not to catch their nerves – they are contagious. Stay calm. Remember live interviews level the playing field between interviewer and interviewee because they cannot be edited, and so you have that advantage over the recorded interview.

Who is the audience?

If you are approached in the street for a vox pop and you give your views to an interviewer on a subject, it is unlikely that you will be thinking about what audience this is for (although there might be a clue in the question: *'what is your favourite children's programme?' 'Should a certain politician resign?'*). However for longer interviews you are advised to think about the audience and how you should address them. As with all media presentation being interviewed is no different in that you should think about whom you are talking to. That way you will best be able to get over clearly what you need to in the most appropriate language – particularly if you are a specialist. While you may be talking to your interviewer it is the audience you are addressing who need to be engaged. Wherever the interview is taking place, do not forget that third party – the audience.

How will the interview be used for broadcast?

You may be interviewed for a variety of formats. They may want a clip for a package, which will be a short feature with at least two clips of interviewees often representing different viewpoints. Both radio and TV do a version of this. You may be approached as part of a vox pop on radio or TV. They may want you for a live interview on radio or TV on daytime programmes. You may be a contributor to a documentary where your contribution will be intercut with others' contributions and other material. You may be interviewed live between several music tracks on a radio music station. You may be part of a studio discussion.

The clip

If the interviewer just wants a 20–30 second clip which will be used in a news piece or feature they should tell you that. In any case it is always advisable to ask what the finished product will be. You will need to think about how you can get your most cogent and attractively packaged message into 20 seconds. You can practise it. Perhaps you are reacting to something surprising that just happened: in any case you may not have time to package your thoughts or pronouncements, in which case the interviewer will do it for you. But the more time you have to think about what you want in the final edit, even though you do not have that choice, the better it will be and easier for the journalist to edit.

The package

What is broadcast from the interview may be just part of one answer you gave the interviewer and it will be almost always without their question. (The exception to this is when only by including a question can they fit in more of what you say that they deem to be important and worth including.) When it comes to editing, skinning a cat comes to mind: there are many ways to do it. Sometimes two clips will be taken from an interview or parts of two answers edited together to make one clip. The finished product – the package – will contain the clip, or clips, 'wrapped' by linking material, and this will not always be presented by the person who interviewed you. Similarly the choice of clips may be made by someone other than the interviewer. So you may feel, watching or listening to the finished product, that it is very different from what you expected. Perhaps the clip they chose, and the angle they take, distort what you originally intended. Also the package may well contain another clip from someone else representing a differing viewpoint which creates an unexpected context for your contribution.

Indeed the purpose of the interview may be to elicit a point of view which you represent (or are thought to) which, in the package, will be balanced by one or more opposing ones. The final edit may contain 20 seconds of you saying that eating red meat is good for you especially accompanied by a glass of red wine, and also 20 seconds from a vegetarian saying all meat is bad for you, and so for that matter is all alcohol. There may also be views from a doctor, a farmer, a nutrionist, etc. What you need to know before the interview is that only 20 to 30 seconds of what you say will be used and, if possible although this is not essential, that your views will probably be balanced by those of others.

Hopefully they will take your most articulate, clearly reasoned contribution. But they are in control of that. And representing your views in the best way is not their responsibility: their role is to choose a clip of the right duration which stands out and serves the whole package well.

Bear in mind that they may well ask provocative questions to elicit a spirited response: *'are you still eating beef after all the health scares? Why?'* Or as Jeremy Paxman might say: *'It's getting a bit embarrassing now, isn't it? Being a Tory/ Labour/Lib Dem supporter/a meat-eater/a Europhile/a global-warming denier'*, etc. Take your pick: make one up for yourself and then answer the question. Your strident defence will make a good clip in a package where opposing views will also feature.

The factual/expert interview

You may be asked for an interview on a subject about which you are expert, or in which you have a particular interest, and they want more than a clip. It may be to do with your position or profession, or your employer's.

You need to know whether your interview is in a sequence and where you are in this sequence. Are you being followed by someone with an opposing view for instance? What has gone before? Is your interview for explanation or perspective, perhaps? You also need to know whether the interviewer is a specialist journalist in your field, what they already know and what angle are they taking. If your field touches on something controversial or in the spotlight then you should be prepared for this. You will need to think about what has been said on the subject already (by colleagues?), which will influence the points you think you should make.

You ought to be able to glean this information in a pre-interview chat with the interviewer or producer. They should give you subject areas that they want to cover, although as said before, they will not want to reveal their definitive questions in advance. They may edit out their questions if it is recorded, but their decision about this and other editing will take place after your involvement with it is finished.

The discussion

If you are invited to take part in a discussion then although the one-to-one nature of the interview has gone, some of the principles remain: that you are involved in a device to elicit information from guests. They will be chosen usually for the diversity of their relationship to the topic, for their professional position, opinion or expertise. What you need to know is where you fit into this, and what is expected of you. Can you imagine being a guest on a discussion about meat?

A chef, a vegetarian (cook or writer), a doctor, a nutritionist and a livestock farmer could have a useful discussion about the benefits of eating meat, meat production, meat and health, the economics of meat versus vegetarianism in various parts of the world as well as other related issues. Perhaps someone who has written a book about meat-eating with a particular angle is a guest. An economist, an anthropologist, a sociologist, even a biologist could all have a contribution to make depending on the angle of the discussion and also the audience.

As one of the guests chosen for your expertise or opinion you can see how you will be able to contribute – the limitations are evident as well as the opportunities. If the discussion is recorded that leaves opportunity for editing. However a producer should only edit for timing and not to alter the bias of the programme favouring one opinion over others. It may be contentious if the producer needs to cut a certain speaker's contribution: the differing positions should remain evident, otherwise there was little point in having the different guests representing them.

The interviewer here is in the role of chairperson who will control the flow, introduce the topic and guests, invite guests to speak, perhaps shut them up too, put questions him/herself, ask other guests to answer questions posed – generally stimulate a debate and then close the proceedings according to time. Everyone should have an opportunity to put their point of view.

The documentary

As a contributor to a documentary your appearance may well be intercut with those of others in the final edited version. But you will probably have been interviewed at length in one go and often on location, at your home or place of work. The location may well be significant (especially on TV) since it will contribute to the story: chef in a busy bustling kitchen, academic in front of book-lined walls, farmer in the fields or farmyard. The background and location themselves are part of the story.

However, you need to know that what you say will be edited (sometimes severely) to fit the overall needs of the programme. You may have your answers ordered according to subject and be broadcast before and after others on the same topic. The sequence of what you say may be altered, the questions no longer there, and other material (recorded, filmed – if TV – or archive) may follow or precede what you say, giving your contribution a context which was not there during the original interview.

I once made a half-hour radio documentary about the quotidian life of a London parish priest knowing that I could effectively intercut a recording of him shouting out bingo numbers in his crypt-cum-bar on Saturday evening with another recording of his intonations at Mass in the church above on Sunday morning. In the final cut there was a slow cross-fade between the two. The distinctly differing ambiences of the two told the story, yet the priest (who was very pleased with the end product) was completely unaware, happily, of my desired contrasting effect as he was being recorded either on the Saturday night or the Sunday morning.

Personality and feature interviews

These kinds of interviews may take place on daytime TV or radio. You could be a guest on a chat show or between tracks on a radio music show. It may be live, or recorded and put together around your choice of music (such as on *Desert Island Discs*). What the interviewer is after here are certain aspects of your life or activities that you are known for; and you will need to know what you can fit into the slot. Very often the producers want anecdotes, funny stories or interesting information about your specialism. You may be invited to answer calls from the public via a phone line into the studio. As with all interviews you should know beforehand what they are likely to be interested in, to be able to best respond. Come prepared therefore with anecdotes or information you know will be welcome.

A well-known actor tells me she appears regularly on daytime TV, both live and recorded. It can be a frustrating experience. Often the researcher will call her and ask some questions and tell her what is expected of her but the interviewer may well ask unexpected questions and sometimes get facts wrong. She says they never want long answers to questions; they do not like you to speak for any length of time. This is tabloid TV: you do not have time to say much of interest. The audience want to see you; they want to hear about the soap's storylines, if you are appearing in one, and they want to see what you look like in 'real life'. In these kinds of interviews appearance is very important.

How to get the best out of an interview

There are a number of factors that will influence the outcome of an interview, some of which you can control, some not. How the interview comes about will influence your performance and how much that performance matters.

Accident or intention?

If you are surprised to be asked to give an interview for whatever reason, you are unlikely to be as prepared than if the initiative to give the interview comes from you. Being asked in the street for your opinions on a subject chosen by the interviewer is likely to produce a different kind of result, and consequently probably matter less, than an interview arranged by you to coincide with the launch of your latest book for example, or even your contribution to a radio phone-in programme. The exception is where you are 'doorstepped' by a journalist who approaches you unexpectedly about something you are connected with and wants a statement. Your response could matter a great deal. You can answer the question unprepared as you are, offer 'no comment', or choose not to respond. (Bear in mind that the last two options may look evasive.) The importance of your reaction depends on the importance of the subject and your connection to it i.e. your authority.

The professionals

If you have access to the expertise of a press or public relations office then you should be guided by them as to how the interview will be conducted: what areas the interview will cover, who is it for, how it will be broadcast, etc. They may even 'hold your hand' during the interview. I have interviewed a government minister who, when asked a question, looked for guidance to his press officer. They discussed the possible answer before recording it, to make sure there were no errors or that a wrong impression could not be given. Such care is necessary for accountable and responsible senior professionals, and if you are representing your company, for instance, then you may need a press officer's help.

'Spin doctors' will try to control the questions and areas of interest in order to put the interviewee in a favourable light. The interviewer may or may not go along with this. Pressure is sometimes applied to stick to pre-arranged questions, or to have a say in the final edit, but good journalists will resist this. Certainly advisers can legitimately try to define the areas of interest, and of course you can always refuse to answer a question if you think you are not qualified to answer it or that it deviates from what was agreed at the outset. You can also refuse to answer if you are asked a personal question, or one which could elicit an embarrassing or libellous response: for example, 'did you sleep with/see money given to the government minister?'

Why are you being interviewed?

You can get a lot of information from the journalist who has approached you. What is the story? What angle are they taking? Why have they approached you in particular? Who else's views have they sought? If they are unwilling to tell you, do they have something to hide? You can of course take your time to agree to be interviewed while you speculate on what is in it for you or your company, and whether you trust the journalist.

Example:

Let us say you are a marine biologist.

EITHER you met someone at a dinner party who took an interest in your subject and who happened to be the friend of a TV producer who was making a wildlife programme and who needed a scientist to explain some irregularities in the reproductive system of whelks in the North Sea. The producer telephones you to discuss your contribution. You wonder whether it is within your field, decide that it is and make an arrangement for the interviewer and crew to come to your home or workplace to do a short interview.

OR the producer may have called the lab where you work and asked to speak to one of the research staff who specialises in North Sea crustaceans, and was referred to you.

In the question that heads this section if the emphasis is put on the 'why' then you may have come to the interview by the first route (the friend of the producer); if the emphasis is on the 'you' then perhaps by the second route (request for a specialist). The answer to the first could be to give scientific weight to the contention that the seas around Britain are becoming polluted and to show the evidence. The second route – the result of better programme research – will produce the answer to help the audience understand how a particular crustacean is affected by certain water conditions.

As an interviewee it is often helpful to know how the interviewer found you in order to assess what he or she wants.

What do they want?

The producer or interviewer may have a very clear idea of what they want from you. They may have expertise themselves and require you to add authority to the thesis or angle of their programme; in which case you can agree to go along with it or suggest another angle or information which they had not thought of. You may compromise. In any case you need to join in the process of deciding what is of interest and what should be included or excluded. Time is always important and it is no good batting on about something you both know will not be relevant. In a recorded interview it will end up on the cutting-room floor or in the digital dustbin.

Of course they may come to you for opinion or an opposing view to one already put (or expected). You need to know this to fulfil that function if it suits you. Make sure they have not got the wrong idea or information, and are expecting something from you that you cannot give.

The message

Politicians are famous for not answering the question. One such once remarked before an interview that he had the answers, all he needed were the questions. This might seem rather a cynical approach and one also that perhaps justifies the rough handling of politicians by certain journalists. But it demonstrates an approach that other interviewees can learn from – namely to define your message prior to interview. What do you want to get across to the audience?

You may like to discuss with colleagues or friends what the top-line message is or the 'headline' of what you want to get over: e.g. *'eating meat is good for you'*, or *'eating red meat is not bad for you if in moderation'*, or *'some crustaceans' sex life is being affected by pollution'*. This helps to keep your focus, especially if the interviewer – intentionally or not – leads you away from what you consider to be the point of the interview.

You will then want to decide on some key points. You cannot rely on the interviewer asking you exactly the right questions especially within a restricted time, so be ready with two or three key points which hopefully you will get to express. If you have anecdotes to illustrate them all the better, since they will capture the audience's attention more effectively. Think of the audience as you make your points so that you avoid jargon or technical language. Make it easy for them.

I am not suggesting you ignore the interviewer's questions. On the contrary, you need to listen to them carefully. But your answers can be on your terms and you can steer the discussion on to your strong ground. You can use phrases such as *'I can best answer that by telling you about'* and insert an anecdote. Or, after briefly answering the question, say: *'but what I think is really important'* or *'the point I would like to emphasise is'* and introduce a key point.

Challenging questions

If the subject of the interview is controversial, the interviewer may want to challenge you or even ask what you may feel are hostile questions. The golden rule is not to get annoyed or emotional. Treat the journalist with respect. Stick to your key points. You can briefly answer a question or ignore it as some do and revert to a key point, as illustrated above, with *'what I think is important here is...'* Be prepared however for the interviewer coming back to what they consider is an unanswered question.

Journalists like to play devil's advocate because it is more interesting for the audience. *'So despite recent research findings you can honestly say that red meat is good for you?'* makes a more provocative, and therefore better question than *'Why do you think red meat is good for you?'* But your answer should remain the same. Stick to your guns and stay calm; do not rise to the interviewer's provocation. It will be counter-productive if you do. They are spicing it up, and you can take advantage of this by answering difficult questions with positive statements: *'Yes I have seen that research and while I agree that if you overdo the red meat you expose yourself to possible health risks, it has also been shown that in moderation red meat is actually beneficial...'*

Keeping control

Remember that although you cannot control the end product, you can of course refuse to take part, or, as is the practice of one well-known politician, record and keep the unedited interview using your own equipment. Having been interviewed by the media before, you may feel that what you say in an interview is distorted by its final treatment in broadcast, and this is one way of checking and importantly showing the journalist that you are watching out for distortion.

SOME PRACTICAL TIPS

As with most presentation, the more experience you gather as an interviewee the better you will become. You will be more relaxed and more able to get what you need across concisely, without diversions, in the most palatable way for your audience. Nevertheless interviewers differ and however skilled you are at answering the questions, you cannot control how they are asked. Inexperienced interviewers can pose particular problems: they may ask the wrong questions or not listen to your answers; they may be nervous or forget the audience. Sometimes there is not much you can do about it. There are, however, some things you can control.

Prior to the interview

We have already discussed the different kinds of interview and you should now know what is wanted, how it will be used, how long, who the target audience is. If you are unclear about any of these, ask. The interviewer is often less available than others, especially if it is live, so a researcher, producer or assistant producer should be there for any queries.

The questions and scope of the interview

It is not usual to be given the questions in advance – except the first one – although you can expect to know what the scope of the interview will be. They will not want to rehearse the interview beforehand, since that will sacrifice the spontaneity when you come to do it for real, and you do not want to be repeating yourself. If there are any areas you would prefer not to deal with then tell the interviewer/producer in advance. If you give a good reason – for instance that you do not have information on that area, or something is undecided – then they should respect that. If they then bring it up during a live interview, it will be either through incompetence (not unknown) or because they think you have something to hide and want to challenge you (see above for your response).

Nerves

If you are nervous, deep breathing helps if you have no time. Even with a few seconds you can breathe into your abdomen on a count of three and out through your mouth on a count of five. Go to Chapter 3 and look at the breathing and relaxation techniques. Focus on the subject of your interview and establish a relationship with your interviewer before the interview starts. Chat about the subject – get into the mode of having a conversation with the interviewer. It will take your mind off your nerves and it may also help to gather important information about what is expected of you.

Checklist

- ✓ Make sure your mobile phone is switched off. The interviewer should have made sure that you are in a quiet environment if not in the studio.
- ✓ If on location any noises (aeroplanes, cars, road works, interruptions) will require you to go back if recording, unless it is acceptable ambient and background noise (perhaps relevant to the subject matter).
- ✓ Make sure you are comfortable.
- ✓ Make sure your volume level has been checked, then you can forget about the microphone and just talk to your interviewer. But do not forget the audience.

For TV

- ✓ Check your appearance. Something you may not have noticed will be magnified on camera. Hair should be tidy (and out of your eyes). If you are in the studio a make-up artist should check you and apply powder if necessary. Men should guard against those shiny receding hairlines! You should be aware that appearance always counts a good deal on TV and can enhance or detract from your message.

- ✓ Be sure to remain still: not slouched if standing, and if seated you should choose a chair that does not move.
- ✓ Check the eye-line between you and the interviewer. If you are of uneven heights make sure that the seating is adjusted so you are not looking up to, or down on the interviewer. The floor staff or crew should see to this.
- ✓ If you have any control over your surroundings – you are at work, in your office for instance – then dress the set. Perhaps a book-lined wall is appropriate, or at the office desk with computer on show. A laboratory or healthcare setting might enhance your message. You may be asked to walk or be filmed doing something connected to your work. Make sure you are comfortable with this. Jacket off or on? Tie? White coat? They all tell a story.
- ✓ A film crew which has come to your place of work to interview you may well want some film of what goes on there. A radio producer may want some sound pictures of the environment to help set the scene. Help them to get what they want and what you want. Make some decisions: what do you want to show them that puts your work in the best possible light to get your message across?
- ✓ Be prepared for the whole process to take time: up to an hour for a 3-minute interview would be entirely normal. The setting-up and technical stuff will take longest, but TV/video never seems to be able to be done in a rush, or if it is, they may want to do it again.

During the interview

It is important to be clear and concise. Try not to ramble. Answer the questions and put your points. We have seen how you can bring the interview onto your strong ground, so make sure you get your key points over.

If the interview is recorded and you do not like your performance – you think you have rambled, gone off the point, on a tangent or for any other reason feel you could give a better answer – then stop and say so. Say that you want to go again.

Be aware however that you cannot overdo this, and that you will lose a certain amount of spontaneity the second time round. The interviewer may counter with their opinion of your performance which they deem satisfactory and that they have already got what they wanted, and that anyway time is short, etc. You cannot bully them. Ultimately they will decide.

The interviewer may also repeat their question if they feel they can get a better answer out of you. If you feel you have answered it already then just repeat what you have said.

For TV

Maintain eye contact with the interviewer on TV, and ignore the camera. If you are in a remote studio, however, look into the lens.

Body language is important. Be careful what you do with your hands. They can be very distracting and send the wrong messages. Keep them away from your face in particular. They can be used for emphasis if it is natural for you to use them, but in general I would keep them down and in front of you.

Phone link

If you are being interviewed via a phone link whether on radio or TV, you are effectively using your phone mouthpiece as a microphone. Make sure you speak clearly, as the sound quality will be lower than if you were speaking into an actual microphone. There are high-quality lines but you would need to be in a studio for that (unless you are a frequent interviewee where you might have an ISDN line installed in your home). Do not have a receiver near you (or turn it right down) when you are speaking on the phone live to a programme, as it will compromise the sound and may produce howl-round – an ugly high-pitched noise.

If you are the caller to a phone-in and you are not used to being 'on air' remember to talk to the presenter as if you were talking to one person on the phone – which in a way you are. Forget about the audience. The art of good broadcasting applies as much to you as the professionals – talk to one person, focus on your material and say your piece, and shut up when you have said it. If challenged, be assertive and stick to your point. If you cannot answer the challenge then come back to your strengths and repeat, if you do not have more to say. The presenter will decide when to move on.

After the interview

You can discuss how it went with your interviewer. They may have different priorities from yours and will be thinking about whether they got what they wanted, rather than your overall performance, especially if it is to be used edited. By all means ask for feedback and advice, but the value of such feedback may be limited, unless your interviewer is also a media trainer. More usefully you can judge your performance on playback and ask yourself whether you got across what you wanted, your key points.

If the interview has been recorded, it is normal for the interviewer or crew to check that it has recorded well, but they will not necessarily invite you to listen or watch a playback especially if they are going to edit it. You can ask for a copy of the finished product which will normally be sent to you after broadcast. Producers frequently promise this and then forget, so make sure you take all their details so you can follow up such a request.

Likewise you can also ascertain when it is likely to be broadcast if it is recorded. But they will not be tied to any answer they give. Follow it up.

SUMMARY

1. Prior to interview you should ascertain certain essentials: is it recorded or live? Who is the target audience? How will the interview be used?
2. The end product could be a clip in a package, a longer factual, expert or feature interview, a discussion or a documentary each with its own very different form.
3. Ask yourself why you are being interviewed, and what the interviewer wants, to get the best out if it.
4. Define your message using key points and anecdotes.
5. Deal with challenging questions evenly, referring to your key points.
6. Find out the scope of the interview.
7. Focus on the subject matter to deal with nerves. Check your appearance for TV. Help create visual aids to put your message across.
8. The interviewer may press you and repeat questions. Equally you can stop and go again if it is recorded. Remember if live you have more control.

The media 10

The application of presentation skills

The presentation skills training that this book offers is for application in today's electronic media. Consequently the presenter and those in front of the microphone and camera need to look at the demands the different media can make on them in order to apply those skills. The fact that those demands change dependent not only on programming fashions, but also on the technologies upon which the different media are based, means that we cannot progress without an interest in technical matters.

New technology brings its challenges and if you, like me, have a tendency to technophobia, remember that what at first sight seems inpenetrable, such as new software, often later becomes indispensable. Sometimes we are simply just afraid of change. It is as well to be aware though that familiarity with current media whims and technological changes will help you to apply your skills.

It is necessary to acquaint yourself with the basics of production techniques and so I include here what I consider to be some of the essential aspects of the media that presenters and their guests will find useful.

Radio, TV, Internet

Some technical aspects of TV and radio are very much the province of technical staff and you will never normally need to know much detail in order to do your job in front of the camera or microphone: sound frequencies, the control room, transmission, equipment purchase for instance. But other parts of the technician's empire will be of interest to you, since they encroach on how you do your job: the microphone, radio desk, camera, autocue, lighting and editing for instance.

The camera and the microphone are intrusive to the unfamiliar performer on TV and radio. Their presence can be a hindrance to a natural delivery, since they remind you that you are not communicating directly with your audience. You may be tempted to get caught up in the 'how' rather than the 'what' – the medium rather than the message. Likewise technicians, studio necessities, the general technicalia can distract you from your 'message'. It is true that with time and experience you will come to feel easier around these necessities. They are particularly prominent in TV since more technical equipment and personnel are necessary for TV production and transmission, whereas radio presentation can and often is done with no one around except the presenter – one of the reasons some people prefer to work in radio.

The Internet offers its own challenges which for us in presentation may be to do with the medium's difference from radio and TV and its audience, which is perhaps more difficult to define and therefore to engage. And yet we must recognise that it may attract those who have never appeared on radio or TV (or perhaps never wanted to), and who now have an appeal that the other media have yet to catch up with. But with YouTube commanding such wide and voluminous attention, those who want to attract some of that attention need to know what the necessary skills are to do that. In some ways the Internet is just a different form of 'publishing' material rather than producing it. And here I include podcasting since it is a form of audio (and video) publishing whose presenters can learn much from the basics of radio (and TV) presentation while retaining their alternative appeal. So there are some technical necessities which remain the same as those in radio and TV production, despite the innovations the Internet has and will go on offering.

I think the best way to deal with the 'necessities' is to understand them as thoroughly as possible in order then to ignore them – to focus more fully on your message. For instance familiarity with the camera can only lead to an easier and more relaxed awareness of its necessity and consequently positive results in front of it.

Let us deal with the different media in turn.

Radio broadcasting

What radio does

Radio technology has been with us for over a century. Radio broadcasting has been with us for rather less. Those of us who work in it, as presenters, defend the medium as one only for the ear since we communicate to our audience by speech without pictures and also assume that the audience will only hear it once. This difference with TV and print media is nowadays frequently compromised by reference to the Internet for the pictures and the ability to hear it again there too. That however requires the listener to do something other than merely listen. Generally radio presentation involves creating the pictures through sound. In this way, paradoxically, radio is a visual medium – a medium for the imagination where visual imagery is stimulated through words and sounds. It is as well to remember that the imagery is personal – the sound is shared but each member of the audience experiences the resultant imagery individually.

The radio market

Radio stations and networks are usually identified and identifiable by their content: talk and phone-ins, news and current affairs, classical, pop, jazz and many other kinds of music. In the UK we know what to expect for instance from BBC Network Radios 4 or 3. For less well known stations on the FM band a regular audience is necessary to justify a station's continuing existence and it is common for stations to close or change their style. On the Internet however the choice is burgeoning where stations have become very specialised.

Looking at the UK radio market some stations offer limited programming but many offer a mix of content: music, news, features, phone-ins, sport, weather, business, arts and other information.

Stations can usually be identified by their intended audience, for instance:

- By age – think of the intended age range of the audiences for BBC Radio 1 and Radio 2 (under 25, and above 35, respectively)
- Or by ethnicity such as BBC Asian Network, Panjab, LGR (London Greek Radio)
- Or by sexual orientation, such as Gaydar.

Local and community stations are identified by area and the communities they serve. Flick the dial in your area to see what is on offer from these smaller stations.

The radio market is even more important to commercial stations which attract a certain audience with a carefully chosen music play-list and programming. The choice of presenter is an essential part of the station's effort to reach that audience. This then will help the marketeers and advertisers to target their products.

Here is an exercise that tries to match presentation style to audience identification:

EXERCISE

Flick the dial or pre-record several radio stations at a certain time of day and see if you can identify the audience they are trying to reach by listening to their presentation. If music is playing, wait till you hear speech or tune in on the top of the hour when there is likely to be a News and other speech just preceding and succeeding it. Think of the age range, gender, and any other grouping. It is too easy to do this with some who identify their audience in the station ID (*'you're listening to Asian Radio'*), with others it is a more subtle exercise. A sidebar of this exercise is that you will come up against strong likes and dislikes. But realise that your dislikes will usually mean you are outside the target audience.

The radio presenter

You can set up a radio station in your bedroom and operate it from there: it may be illegal but it is simple. Internet-streamed radio often features only music – no presenters. In these days of blogging and podcasting, simplicity of operation is attractive. But if you want to gain and retain listeners then you have to give them something they want. In this sense radio is nearer to its consumers. It not only feels it when, at best, the presenter seems to be having a conversation with the listeners, but also when the presenter leaves the studio to go and actually meet them. Or when they are out and about with portable or outside broadcast equipment. Community and local radio encourage this when they try to fulfil their role in the community defined geographically by the area the signal reaches, which varies in size but is often quite small.

RADIO TECHNICAL MATTERS

In general you will have to familiarise yourself with more technical stuff in radio than in TV since it is less technically complicated and specialised and so can be operated by fewer people. In these days of labour cut backs and freer unionised practice, what was once done by three people can now be done by one – and that often includes the presentation! So if you want to present on radio it is wise to learn how to operate and edit. What you will need to familiarise yourself with in radio will include:

- The microphone
- Operating a radio desk
- Portable recording equipment (for interviews and location broadcasts)
- The operation of digital editing software.

Microphone technique

Microphones command respect. For instance if you move your head away from the mic on radio then you will not be heard, or your level will drop unacceptably. If you are too close it will distort. Understand its needs and then forget it – in order to speak beyond it to your audience. As a performer on radio you will sometimes have the luxury of a studio manager or sound engineer, but it is advisable to become familiar with technical operations as many presenters 'self-op' (operate the equipment themselves while broadcasting).

There are a range of mics which do different things. Studio mics come in several shapes and sizes. Although different ones are suitable for different set ups – single use, interviews, discussions, etc. – the decision will normally be the sound engineer's. And if you are working with studio managers or sound engineers then they will satisfy themselves that you are the correct distance from the mic and will take level and point out any problems such as 'popping'.

Popping occurs when you make plosive sounds (e.g. *p*'s and *b*'s), and they cause a magnified 'pop' which you will hear either through your headphones or when you play the recording back or even on transmission if you have not noticed it before. It will mar the output.

It is as well, though, to be able to know how to deal with this yourself. If you are popping it may be because you are too close or speaking too directly into the mic, so that the air from your mouth produces this unwanted sound. You can adjust the mic so that you are speaking to it indirectly – tilted or slightly at an angle. This will only be possible with some mics and the sound engineers if available will help. But if on your own you will need to find out what works best.

Likewise taking level is easy enough to do on your own and a necessity, since if your level is either too high or low it will seriously mar your broadcast. On a meter the needle should be ideally $5\frac{1}{2}$ for speech and $4\frac{1}{2}$ for music. Peaking at 6 or over usually produces distortion, and 4 and below probably means you are off-mic and therefore unacceptably low. If you are self-opping you should keep an eye on this meter as you present. On a scale of lights the level of the lights reflects the recording level and they usually show red when the level is too high but remain in green if the level is ok.

Do not be tempted to get too close to the mic. About 6 to 10 inches (15 to 25 cm) in a radio studio should be about right. Any closer and you are inviting the listener to hear unwanted sounds such as lip smacking, saliva, popping, sibilance and heavy breathing. Some people work closer to the mic for certain effects – greater intimacy, for example. In drama you can create the feeling that you are inside the listener's head. This is unsuitable for most broadcast work. And remember that the distance to the mic mirrors the distance to the listener – which is important. In a lot of presentation the effect you are after is that of having a conversation with an acquaintance. You do not want to invade their personal space – we all know what it is like when someone we do not know does that. And yet you do not want to be remote; just close enough to make an impact.

Microphones are very sensitive and pick up unwanted signals. You can often tell if someone is nervous on mic – they emit very subtle but betraying noises from their upper chest. The mic is more revealing than the camera. It is easier to lie on TV than on radio. An experiment carried out to establish just that demonstrated that it was easier to mask inner thoughts on camera by being poker-faced than by trying to do the same on mic which discloses more than mere words. It is as well to be aware of this. If you are tired for instance, or preoccupied, but think you are covering it up on radio, the chances are you are not. Listen carefully to your ROTs (recording off transmission) to confirm this.

Headphones

You will have to wear headphones ('cans') for some radio broadcasting, and it is as well to get used to them. They can distract you, as you hear your own voice through the equipment, and affect your delivery, but you can also learn to use them to aid you. As you get used to them they can help you judge your level, and give you some idea of how you are going out on air. With live radio broadcasting you need them so that people can communicate with you. If you are in the studio with others and the mics are live then it is through your headphones that producers or studio managers can talk to you without them going out on air or cutting the mics. Producers and studio managers should not talk to you in your cans while you are broadcasting – it will distract you and mar your performance. Sometimes it is unavoidable – if there is an emergency for instance, such as 'don't read the next story – it's libellous!' Some presenters become adept at dealing with this distraction especially in fast-moving live programmes – sport for example.

When I train presenters I often encourage them not to wear headphones to try to get a more conversational or natural delivery. Sometimes you will see presenters wearing one on and one off, so they keep in touch with studio and output but strive for better delivery without hearing themselves. As a guest on a radio programme you will not normally be required to wear them, nor will they be offered.

On your own in a self-op radio studio you need to be able to hear yourself on headphones. You can monitor the level and watch out for popping.

Radio desks

If you have ever been in a radio or recording studio the desk can look like a formidable even intimidating piece of equipment. It can contain rows of channels with a myriad array of buttons, and nowadays an increasing number of computer screens. Presenters and radio guests will never need to know how to operate these larger desks, which offer sophisticated sound management necessary for the multi-track recording and broadcasting of some music and drama. Smaller versions or parts of these larger desks are all that is necessary for speech-based or simple music programming. And if you have to operate the desk yourself as presenter (self-op) then it will have to be presenter-friendly. Nevertheless you will need to familiarise yourself with each desk you self-op and make sure you can operate the equipment efficiently while also focussing on what you are saying – whether reading or ad-libbing.

The basic elements of a radio desk are:

- Channels with fader controls
- Level meter(s) or rows of lights
- EQ (equalisation) buttons
- Pan-pot
- Gain control
- Pre-fade buttons
- Loudspeaker and headphone volume and balance controls.

Channels with fader controls

Each channel can be connected to a different sound source such as CD player, microphones, other studios, audio feeds from elsewhere, phone lines, mini-disc player, computer software audio, etc. – the possibilities are numerous. The channel is operated by a fader control which goes either up or down according to a station's protocol. As they are moved away from the backstop then the level is increased. Some at the BBC are off when up and open downwards, whereas most in the industry are closed when down and move up to open.

Level meter(s) or rows of lights

The level meter will sometimes be needles, and usually two needles for stereo, in a window measuring 1 to 6 or 7 (this is standard at the BBC). It may, however, be indicated by two rows of lights which will be in green until they go over the normal limits, and then will be in red. With the needles a red light usually indicates the level is too high.

EQ (equalisation) buttons

EQ buttons will cut or boost frequencies to change the output. Presenters use them to give themselves more bass or alter their voices in other ways. How to improve your sound using equalisation is really the province of expert sound engineers and I advise you to leave well alone unless you are with an experienced technician. By all means play with them to see what they can do, but be careful about using them for broadcast.

Pan-pot

These buttons place the sound to the left or right in the stereo range.

Gain control

This boosts the volume in the channel with increased amplification. You can use them to set level, and so when the fader is fully open you will know that you have the correct level.

Pre-fade buttons

These allow you to hear a channel output through the speakers or headphones without you actually opening that channel. If you want to hear what you sound like on mic without interrupting what is going out, press the pre-fade button on your mic channel and you can not only hear yourself but also take level by using the gain or fader controls and reading your level on one of the meters usually labelled 'pre-fade level'.

Loudspeaker and headphone volume and balance controls

This allows you to control the volume coming through the speakers and headphones. It will not affect the output level going out through the channels. Music presenters (deejays) often like the headphones turned up loud – it's a matter of preference – likewise the speakers. The studio loudspeakers will be cut automatically when the mic fader is opened, otherwise you would get howl-round – a high-pitched noise which is a sort of sound short-circuit. The headphones, however, will not cut out when you open the mic and so you can still monitor the output through them.

Portable recording equipment

A lot of radio content can and is recorded on location by using portable equipment. Outside and location broadcasting is also possible by radio car or OB van. In the latter case you would have technical help, in the former case you would also probably have technical help with you or if not be given training as to how to operate the equipment.

Radio stations' use of portable recorders is changing and at the moment small hard-drive recorders are the popular choice. They sometimes have a removable memory card which might be useful for storage if you are doing a number of interviews or recordings (for a documentary for example). You need to have a good-quality microphone with you too, as the sound quality will be determined by that. And if you are outside you will need a wind shield on the mic to minimise the effects of wind and other unwanted ambient sound.

You can bring the recorder back to the studio to play or dub (record) through a desk or transfer the recording straight into a computer for editing via a WAV file – an audio computer file. Alternatively you can transfer the recording to a laptop and edit on location and send back the finished product by FTP (File Transfer Protocol) via the Internet.

If you are doing interviews using portable equipment always make sure you know how to use it before you go. Make sure the battery is fully charged or you have spare ones with you. And before you dismiss your interviewee, make sure you have the recording by checking it through its speaker or headphones. I have had some embarrassing moments with technical problems on my equipment, when I had to keep VIP interviewees waiting while I sorted them out.

Editing for radio

Digital editing using computer software is not difficult. There are a number of software editing packages. Pro Tools and Audition seem to be dominant at the moment. Having mastered the technical know-how you then have to think about how best to edit your recorded material for broadcast, and that will depend on what the end product is going to sound like. Editing on quarter-inch tape with razor blade and chinagraph pencil has all but disappeared, but like all previous technologies it holds not only a nostalgia for those of us who used them, it also taught the basic principles, in this case, of editing. One advantage with digital editing, however, is that it allows you to keep the original so you can make several versions, and if you make a mistake you can always start again.

Multi-track editing, where audio from different sources are mixed together, becomes possible and music editing can also be easily done when you know how. In fact there are a lot of possibilities with digital editing that were not on offer in one box, as it were, with analogue. You just have to learn how.

TELEVISION

A glance at any comprehensive TV listings magazine shows what is on offer in the UK. The channels have multiplied in a generation. This is partly due to the technological changes with satellite, cable and digital offering more choice and with it differing ways of paying for it. The licence fee which funds the BBC still stands, but seems often under pressure as other networks take audience share but are funded by subscription, advertising or a mixture of the two. More changes in technology and funding are bound to come, and perhaps what is on offer now will hardly be recognisable in another generation. High-definition and rectangular screens are recent innovations which have an impact on presentation with a need for sophisticated make-up and changes to how you are framed.

But with more channels come more opportunities for those in the industry and if you look through the listings you can perhaps identify some programming areas which could offer an opening suited to your interests. Although there are now many different channels, the skills remain the same. The BBC has had a good tradition of training and those skills can be applied industry-wide, but many people also come in from other media and indeed from outside the industry and make good in a business which lives on ideas – often recycled ones and even repeated ones – which only work if they catch and keep the viewers' attention.

TELEVISION AND VIDEO PRODUCTION

Television and video production whether in the studio or on location is technically more complex than radio and the finished product is less dependent on the presenter and more on the pictures to tell the story. If as presenter or guest you are involved in the production or choice of these pictures then the more involved you will feel to be. But often you will come in at a later stage to fulfil your part of the production and may feel therefore a smaller part of finished product.

It will be easier to understand the demands of TV for the presenter and guest if we look at:

- Who does what?
- Some TV programming
- Outside broadcasting
- Autocue
- Recording tracks
- Some basic tips.

Who does what?

There always seem to be endless personnel in a TV environment. Different kinds of production with different budgets employ differing numbers of people. Even in the select area of a live TV programme studio. There can for instance be strand editors and editorial assistants, whose jobs I have not included here. Look at the credits on a TV programme and you have some idea of who is involved and then there are many more who do not merit a mention. Here is a non-exhaustive list of some of the essential personnel you are likely to work with (sometimes indirectly) as presenter or guest.

- **The programme editor** is the boss. They control the budget and will be carrying out the plans of the commissioners or controllers. They have overall editorial control of the programme. They hire and fire and ultimately decide who and what is in the script and therefore the programme.

- **The producer** has editorial control over the programme. They are responsible for what goes into a particular edition. Timing is very important in live TV and the producer, with the director, decides when items must be cut or allowed to run on. They will also have to decide what to do when things go wrong. *Assistant producers* may be assigned parts of the programme (in daytime live TV for instance where there are several different segments).

- **The director** supervises what goes on and when, during a shoot or programme recording, putting script to screen. In a live programme such as news, sport, business or daytime TV, the director is responsible for how the presenter(s) and guests look on the screen. They communicate with the camera operators, choosing the shots offered by them. They are responsible for the graphics and captions, getting film clips inserted, dealing with outside lines and circuits, instructing the vision mixer and carrying out the editorial decisions of the producer, as well as liaising with the floor manager and presenter (the latter through their earpiece). Together with a lighting or technical manager they may also decide on how the set is lit.

- **The camera operator** is on the studio floor with a shot list and/or doing what the director asks of them. They will also offer shots which the director can accept or ignore. Sometimes in a small news studio robot cameras are operated remotely or are simply fixed. These cameras can zoom, tilt, pan, go up and down and focus.

- **The floor manager** is also on the floor of the studio and liaises between the director in the gallery and the presenter and guests in the studio. With the *assistant floor manager* (*AFM*) they will usher guests in and out and on a busier set deal with a studio audience, cue the presenters and generally manage what goes on in the studio.

- **The vision mixer** operates the desk and monitors and therefore determines what goes on the screen, following the director's wishes. This role can be done by the director in a small studio. Vision mixing is in effect editing live.

- **The picture editor** operates an editing suite that knits together pictures and sound to make short packages for news programmes. If you are putting together a package you will need to choose clips from what is available and write and voice a track over some of them. The picture editor will put it together for you respecting the slot size and the sometimes short period of time you have to do it in.
- **The sound engineer** as you might expect, looks after the sound and also answers to the director. The engineer is in the gallery with the director controlling all sound from its various sources. Presenters and guests are usually mic-ed up with clip-ons. They may be radio or cabled. Occasionally a boom is used if there are too many people to mic up or questions are being taken from an audience. Alternatively a directional or 'gun' mic might be taken to whoever is speaking. These latter two require people to operate them, of course.
- **Others** include the *graphics producer* who looks after graphics, and *operator* to play them and other inserts (e.g. film, video recordings) into the broadcast. The *script runner* is the junior who does all the odd jobs.

TV programming

The schedules of the important networks involve the sharp edge of getting and keeping audiences and it is the business of highly paid executives to make sure that those audiences are served. The presentation of the programmes are part of that, and if a presenter can deliver an audience then his or her salary and employment prospects move northwards to reflect their appeal. This is the crossover between presenting and celebrity appeal. But fashions change, and right now property and cooking shows seem to be all over the schedules and quiz shows may be fading. Reality TV may also be on the wane, but 24-hour news is holding up, as are confessional and family heartache audience programmes. Who knows what the schedules will look like in five years' time. Different, for sure.

On satellite and digital there are whole channels devoted to history, science, shopping, geography, fashion (home and clothes) and, of course, numerous channels offering children's programmes and sport.

The personnel, the studio, the location and the presentation will all change according to the type of programme and how it is filmed. In general from the point of view of those in front of the camera you will be there because of your expertise and knowledge of the subject matter; and, of course, because the camera, the executives and the audience like you. You will get used to the set-up as it is in your area of expertise. Let us look at some of those programme/subject areas:

- News
- Sport
- Business
- Weather
- Daytime and lifestyle
- Children's
- Continuity.

News

A news studio is just that – a studio dedicated to news. In some ways it is the simplest set-up, especially as found in regional news studios where neither set nor lighting change, since the presenter and guests (if there are any) tend to be in the same place, and all that goes on is talking either to camera or between presenter and guest(s) including other journalists. Recently in the UK, particularly on network news programmes, newscasters have started to present standing up, with or without a desk and occasionally moving around which will involve keeping an eye on which camera is live. They will also have to take their script with them. They will, however, usually be seated for an interview.

News is always transmitted live and the relationship between presenter and director is vital since changes and updates can happen at any time. With live interviews in the programme you have to keep an eye on the timings. Much can and does go differently from plan because of various unforeseen problems: circuits and lines in and out of the studio acting unpredictably for example, or guests turning up late or even not showing up at all. The news is read off autocue which I will deal with below.

One or two of the cameras may be static and/or operated remotely (from the gallery), so you may be on your own in the studio without camera operators or floor management. You may also be located in the newsroom itself with all the bustle around you to give the viewer an idea of the industrious environment in which the news is compiled.

Sport

In some ways sport is like news only more so. Sport has an energy which is also reflected on the technical side with commentaries and location interviews, and film inserts. The sports news presenter often joins the news presenter(s) at the end of the news and does a similar job as the newscaster introducing film inserts, interviewing and reading to camera via autocue.

Sports commentary at the venue is a specialised activity where boxes are reserved for commentators (radio and TV). They often use 'lip-mics' – hand-held mics with a ridge at the top so that you speak right into them to give your presentation priority over the inevitable background noise. They may, however, use mic and headphone headsets. They are always out of shot. An outside broadcast van (OB) will often accompany such live presentations.

Business

Business has become more important, with financial market and economic news commanding more interest outside the City. As with sport, a dedicated presenter will follow the news and do the same job. There is a tendency for more graphics with business and now also more standing and moving around.

Dedicated business programmes, like sports programmes, are transmitted live and can be on the hairy side with lots of live feeds coming in, live interviews and changing scripts and so require an anchor who responds well to last-minute direction. Guests too (if you are one) need to remain calm in this kind of stressful atmosphere.

Weather

TV forecasters are often in a dedicated studio. They will have meteorological expertise, and have contact with the Weather Centre. They will also reflect the editorial consistency of the network. The technology involves a screen onto which is projected computer images allowing the viewer to see the charts. The forecaster will see a faint image of them so that they can point out particularities. They control the sequence which will fit with the words which will not usually be scripted (nor therefore read from autocue). They will also have to tailor (often during the broadcast) the timing to a changing slot dependent on what the news have allowed for. A network director who controls continuity and therefore also the weather slot usually controls timings.

Daytime and lifestyle

Programming during the day offers (as on radio) a lot of opportunities for presenters and guests. Look at the listings to see what is currently in vogue. At the time of writing property and auction shows seem to be prevalent as well as the studio-based double-headed presenter-led lifestyle shows. Teams of production staff manage this programming. The technical necessities will be handled by dedicated personnel and you will only have to master your script through your expertise – journalistic or otherwise. Animation and enthusiasm are qualities which TV like (producers and audience), and so alongside those assets you will need to become familiar with the necessities of the studio or a location shoot.

Children's

Whole channels are devoted to children's programming. That which is studio based will require from the presenters lots of energy and an almost theatrical style – indeed many children's presenters have come from an acting background. Presenting to children requires an appeal which is quite specialised. It is important not to patronise, and have an instinct for what works and more importantly perhaps what does not. You could be working with animals as well as children in the studio both of which will require special attention, as their behaviour can be unpredictable.

Continuity

A TV channel's transmission suite which puts the programme stream to air will also have a continuity sound booth for the announcer to voice linking material. The material the viewer sees between programmes will include channel idents (a reminder of what channel you are watching), promotions, trails for future programmes and commercials. A lot of this will usually have been produced using independent production and voice-over talent. Continuity announcers are needed for live linking and are skilled at reading to time over the credits of finishing programmes, channel and network idents and other linking visual material.

If you listen to these links you will notice how the voice-over is part of the identity of the channel. Part of what continuity is doing is trying to keep the audience with that channel. Network directors and those who cast those voices will be thinking about an audience who identify with their continuity style.

Outside broadcasting

Filming away from the studio can offer extra challenges for the presenter. You may well be more involved in the process to get what is necessary either live or recorded, as you will be interacting with your environment and more an active part of the team. Depending on your relationship with the camera man or woman you may be able to control what shots will be framed. They may take your suggestions and you might have to take theirs.

The team will be small – it may be sound camera and presenter. Or just camera and presenter. Or indeed solo – video journalists do it all by themselves: camera, sound and presentation. It leaves you with less scope but the training should show you what is possible. Zooming and camera movement would seem to be out in a piece to camera, but there are ways round that if you have helpful by-standers!

If you do have a crew, you will need to rehearse the part of your script you deliver on camera while they are setting up. Do you learn it? Do you paraphrase? Can they write it on boards behind the camera? Some presenters use an autocueing device which is self-operating, so that the pre-recorded script is played into your ear piece as you present – you will have to contend with hearing the recording at the same time as you are speaking – not an easy skill to master. There is also sometimes the possibility of autocue on location.

You may be required to walk and talk, to hit marks and be precise about where you are in relation to the camera, to come in to or out of shot and to acknowledge the natural light (or lack of it). You may also have to deal with the unexpected (especially if live). There will be technical problems so that you will have to do re-takes (sometimes many) even if your performance was fine: you may feel the one they use was not your best.

News OBs

If you are reporting on location for News and Current Affairs there are a number of challenges you may have to face, according to programme, budget, time available as well as all the usual ones such as weather conditions, available interviewees and co-ordinating with the other members of the team. Here are some scenarios that will directly affect your presentation:

- The producer wants to change your script – you have to re-learn it or find a way of presenting the new script without much time to rehearse.
- You need to change your script because of latest developments but the new script does not fit strict timing necessities. You need to cut or lengthen at very short notice.
- If you receive a 'throw' from the studio anchor (such as *'what's the latest, Jim... ?'*) and you are doing a 'dough-

nut' i.e. interviewing several people in turn with links by you before you hand back to studio, you have to monitor what has preceded you in the studio so that you do not repeat anything already said. But if nothing was said, you have to ad-lib an introduction to the subject with little or no notice.

- You are doing a two-way with the studio and they ask supplementary questions which have not been pre-arranged.

Qualities necessary for location presenting

Presenters are often valued for their flexibility and ability to perform under pressure (especially of time) and in spite of technical problems. As more is out of your control on location then you will often have to compromise. Essential qualities must include:

- being a good team player so that you understand others' professional concerns
- being adaptable to change – if you have a fixed idea how you want a shot to work and it needs to be abandoned for reasons outside your control you immediately adapt to plan B (and there always will be a plan B)
- keeping focus on material and audience while coping with unfavourable location, weather, technical conditions (e.g. there's a howling wind, an aeroplane overhead, a disruptive passer-by, five minutes to go, etc.).

Autocue

Mastery of autocue is an essential for live TV presenting. It is also used occasionally on location and for recorded TV and video shoots. It allows you to speak straight into camera and read the scrolling script projected onto the camera lens, giving the impression that you are talking to the viewer rather than reading a script. It takes a little practice but is not difficult to master. It can and is sometimes self-operated by a pedal or hand, but it is often operated by a technician either in the studio or gallery who will scroll according to the speed you are speaking.

At first you may panic that the words will disappear off the top of the frame before you have had time to read them, but that should not happen. If you slow down, the scroll will go slower; likewise if you speed up, it will go quicker.

Another problem is the size of font, since the camera may be some five metres from you. If the font is too big there will not be space to fit much on the screen, and you will more easily be inclined to lose the sense of what you are reading. It is therefore important that you have pre-read the script so that you know what is coming up. And watch out for cues to video, film or sound which will be indicated in the script although not for reading out obviously.

If you are co-presenting, then you may be sharing the autocue – your part should be initialled.

Occasionally the autocue breaks down during a live broadcast when you will have to refer to your hard copy which you should have in front of you or to the script on your computer screen. In order to successfully transfer to this you will need to have turned over the scripts, or scrolled, as you go.

Reading from hard copy to camera will involve holding it up slightly so that you do not have to look down too much giving the viewer too much top of head. And try to practise looking at the script and then delivering a good chunk of text straight to camera.

Recording the track

Laying down a track is putting words to the pictures. You record your script usually with the video/film playing on a monitor in front of you. But first you may have to write the script. That is a particular skill that requires care and practice. The pictures in essence tell the story – but not on their own. And you will need to fit words to the pictures that do not just tell you what the viewer can see. There will be natural sound to the pictures, some of which is essential, some desirable and some faded under or lost altogether to accommodate your voice-over.

Be prepared to edit your script down to its bare essentials (and to have it edited by others). Write short sentences in the first place but also get used to paring down a script. The script should be simple, not over-written, bearing in mind that good pictures convey lots of information themselves and viewers become confused if the script is in conflict with the pictures or demands too much attention. In any case the words need to be timed exactly to fit the pictures.

You may be recording the track sitting next to the picture editor using a lip-mic, which is used in an environment of low-level surrounding sound. A lip-mic is not as sensitive as the mics used in a sound booth where you could be working in front of your own monitor showing the footage. You have to work a bit harder with a lip-mic otherwise you will sound a bit flat.

And what of the difference between radio broadcasting and voicing over TV pictures? With radio you have more of the audience's attention. With TV because the pictures are telling the story you are supplementing them. Think about where you are spatially in relation to the audience. In radio you are facing them, but with TV voice-over you are more at their side as they watch the pictures, popping the information into their ear.

If you are reporting from a location where you may have done a piece to camera it is important that the track reflects that you are there – not in a studio where you may be recording the track. You need to think yourself back into the scene that you can see on your monitor. It of course depends on the pictures, but it is as well to think about your relationship to the scene on the screen and how you address your audience.

Some general tips

There is not room here to provide you with a comprehensive guide to television and video production. Take any opportunity to talk to professionals in the medium, as they will have useful tips. Here are some.

- Take a lot of interest in your appearance and wardrobe:
  - Hair is very important on camera. It should above all be tidy, and appropriate (a relative term I know: if uncertain take advice).
  - Some colours do not work on camera. Best avoid strident checks and patterns. Dark greens and navy blues turn to black. Some colours better suit particular individual's colourings.
  - TV make-up allows for the draining effect of TV studio lighting.
- Practise putting your material over using gesture. Some gestures help get the information across. Watch pieces to camera (PTCs). Notice what the size of camera-frame allows. Be careful about bringing your hands into close contact with your face – not usually a good idea.
- Television allows for fewer nuances than radio, and so some think it a more superficial medium. The script needs to be simple and direct – subtleties are sometimes lost.
- Get your audience's attention from the start. You can hang a PTC on a flourishing turn of phrase.
- Energise on camera. Think about your on-screen persona. One presenter describes himself as having 'a beam of low-key goodwill'; as being 'seraphic, equable and affable'.
- Rehearse your script out loud to see how it sounds.
- Think about taking the viewers through your text at a pace, and with a logical structure they are going to understand.

THE INTERNET

Of the recent media innovations offered via the Internet two stand out – one video, one audio – YouTube and podcasting. That is not to say they will remain the dominant applications for the presenter. Who knows what will be on offer in even a few years' time. Many sites offer audio and video material the presentation of which matters as much as it does on radio and TV. The defining and unique quality of what the Internet has to offer is its accessibility – it is open to a different, larger, more diverse group of people than radio and TV, both consumers and contributors. And its special qualities are influencing changes in the older media: blogging, reality TV, streaming Internet radio, podcasting, interactivity, to name a few.

Nevertheless, much as it impresses, the Internet also demonstrates one quality which endears itself more to its users than to TV and radio professionals: its lack of editorial control. Anybody and anything can get onto the Internet, and that poses a problem. How do we value it? Before I address that, I should qualify my sweeping statement as large parts of the world have restricted access to the Internet either because of inadequate telecommunications or government control, but their access or lack of it will not change the Internet's nature; at least not in the (US-dominated) short term.

I propose to deal with:

- Webcasting
- YouTube
- Podcasting.

Webcasting

A webcast is broadcasting audio or video via the Internet. The reception of this material varies widely, and therein lies its main difference from conventional broadcasting via audio and video receivers: quality. Erosion of quality is more of a problem with video material: there may be delay as the pictures catch up with the sound, and the picture quality is sometimes poor. This is due to a number of factors which vary according to equipment and connection. In future as technology progresses so will quality. Poor quality, however, does have an effect on presentation.

The video frame on a computer screen can usually be measured in centimetres whereas the size of modern TV screens is now fractions of metres. Widescreen is becoming the norm for TV, but the portrait-shaped box is probably how the viewer will see you framed on their computer.

Getting the message across becomes a more uphill task, since your audience will be more difficult to engage. The message needs to be clear, concise and focussed. There will be less room for nuance, humour or subtlety. The same is true of video conferencing where a meeting can take place via a video link at several locations (worldwide if necessary). But just as there are of course important differences between video conferencing and meeting in person, you need to recognise the limitations of webcasting.

Nevertheless, TV and radio stations are putting more and more material on their websites as they want to reach the on-line audience which is potentially huge. BBC Online (a worldwide favourite) is now regarded as an increasingly important part of BBC output, and their (and other broadcasters') video and audio material is accessible throughout the world. Also the facility of watching TV and listening to radio programmes repeated on the web, after they have been broadcast traditionally, is increasingly popular.

A presenter has only to observe the principles in this book to appear as successfully via the web as on TV and radio. Perhaps the message that you are putting across can take precedence over engagement with the audience for the simple reason that the audience is potentially vast and therefore unknowable. Not that that should deter you from trying to engage them. Finding out who they are is difficult – even more so than the audience of a worldwide broadcaster – but if that does not deter advertisers trying to reach them it should not deter presenters either.

YouTube

YouTube is a video-sharing website where users can upload and share video clips. The site has been an Internet phenomenon and recognised and used by millions worldwide. The appeal is universal, anyone can contribute and they do, and thus contributors range from the seriously talent-free to Hollywood superstars. But therein lies its appeal since those with already immense media exposure feel the need to be on there as much as those the other media ignore. US presidential candidates use it as do aspiring indie music bands. Like the Internet itself YouTube appeals without reference to cultural, national, age or any other divide. It offers something for everyone.

It attracts video bloggers (or vloggers) who can reach an audience denied them elsewhere in the media, but without editorial controls they offer the audience limited value and little competition to radio and television. A lot of content is at best mediocre. By the same token, however, users go to YouTube for what they cannot find in the conventional media. A lot of *popular* content (flagged up as such) is fresh, witty, eye catching, oddball, talented and sometimes frankly superior to traditional media content.

For presenters therefore it offers an opportunity: for trial and error, to showcase, and in general air material refused by traditional media outlets. If you are full of ideas here is a possible outlet for them with a potential audience of millions. In general it would seem the audience is young, and will reward the innovative over the polished. This is not to say that you should ignore what has been offered in this book, since those principles apply to innovators as much as they do to the old school.

Podcasting

Podcasts are files usually downloaded from the Internet, which can be transferred to an MP3 player, iPod, mobile phone and other portable devices for playing on the move. Typically they contain only audio but increasingly also visual and video material. Podcasts are often published in episodes and downloaded automatically to subscribers; however they can be listened to and watched via a computer like a webcast without being downloaded and transferred to a portable device.

The subject matter is very varied, encompassing everything that is already broadcast via TV and radio, and much more besides, catering for every interest. Increasingly newspapers and magazines are using the form to offer what can sound like a radio version of their titles. It is now possible to hear what *The Guardian* or *The New York Times* sound like. There is also education, entertainment, music, comedy, sport, science, arts, health and religion, to mention a few. If you have the application iTunes it is easy to find out what is on offer via iTunes>Store>Podcasts. Although Apple developed the technology, podcasts are also available via Windows.

There are easily accessible tutorials both in audio and text form on how to make a podcast. What is often left out of the manuals, however, are any tips on presentation, which varies widely. If you bear in mind that the podcast will be heard (or viewed) at a later date, for instance on the train to work on a portable player (such as an iPod), you will appreciate that care needs to be taken. It is not live and it needs to be crafted. It is a production.

Music, video effects and technical sophistication can make a podcast attractive, but as far as presentation goes much of what applies to radio pertains here too. What is exciting is that material is reaching a new audience via an audio form, and hitherto text-only material is finding a wider audience via this medium. For instance an art gallery can display not only its pictures but relay criticism, history and interviews with artists and curators to a remote audience. Podcasting is ideal for language learning since it offers short episodes of audio-only tutorials. And if whatever is heard or seen on a podcast is necessarily a short form – typically five minutes – it encourages an enthusiastic audience to purchase a more comprehensive version. Here the presenter is helping to sell.

TRANSFERABLE MEDIA PRESENTATION SKILLS

Although you will become practised as well as familiar with that corner of the media that employs you most, attaining a general skill set is not only possible but desirable to allow your abilities to be transferable. Ask presenters and look at their CVs. They move from TV to radio and vice versa, taking in corporate work, voice-overs and writing. They may do the shopping channel one day and a radio music-presenting shift the next. There is a growing market out there with the expansion that digital TV and radio offer. In short broadcasting via TV, Radio and the Web are not the only home for your presentation expertise.

Other media communication

There is not space to discuss in detail presentation in all media forms. Here are some which you may come across and indeed become professionally involved with:

- Audio books.
- Self-help audio.
- Therapy and hypnotism by audio.
- The shopping channels.
- Audio description of theatre and TV for the blind.
- Magazines and other textual material for the blind.
- Audio guides in galleries, museums, monuments and buildings.
- Audio and video safety guides.
- Dedicated traffic and weather radio and TV.
- Language learning audio and video.
- Translation and interpretation audio service.
- Public address announcements live or recorded.
- Internet radio streaming.
- Telephone and video conferencing.

SUMMARY

1. Technical necessities in media although essential can intimidate. Become familiar with what you need to know technically and then focus on *your* necessities.
2. Who is listening to you? Identify your radio market.
3. Mic, desk, headphones, portable equipment and editing software are radio essentials – learn how to use them.
4. Who does what in the team in a TV environment? You need to know.
5. Become familiar with what's popular on TV. Watch and learn.

6. Location filming requires flexibility and skills as a team player.
7. Autocue needs practice to master. As does the writing and recording the track to TV pictures. You will pick up tips as you go.
8. YouTube crosses over with mainstream media, but is freer of editorial control. It is exciting and attracts a huge audience. What can you offer it?
9. The popularity of podcasts is growing. Although a wider range of material can be offered via podcasts, its similarities with radio include presentation skills.

Final thoughts 11

USEFUL QUALITIES NOT IN THE JOB DESCRIPTION

What qualities, other than those related to their expertise, do good presenters display? I have often found that those presenters easiest to work with are the ones whom the audience responds well to, and so who are also good at their jobs. They are good under pressure. The environment is not always an easy one where stress, hierarchies, pettiness and even bullying are not unknown. I once had a colleague who joined a very high-profile current affairs programme as a junior reporter, and who told me that the only person in the team who would even talk to her and was pleasant was the presenter, who ironically gives the impression *on air* of being the proverbial semi-house-trained polecat. He can humiliate politicians, but he is good to work with.

Being a team player

A presenter is a member of a team, and if he or she has the time, usually because they are on top of what they are doing, they may make a point of being personable with their colleagues and also importantly with the guests, who feel, and therefore work, all the better because of it. However there are the difficult ones for whom the stress and demand for high standards take their toll. Egos are exposed and they have to be managed. It can be testing especially when people are tired or working long unsocial hours. Team management should be high on an editor/producer's list of priorities.

Talent

Some people will naturally shine on camera or easily project personality on mic, but talent should not be a major concern for you. Let others speculate – even decide. Those that review, employ, promote, produce, direct, judge, even train (although it is unhelpful), can make talent their business. You have something more important to get on with. It will not be helpful if your focus is on your individual ability rather than the material you are putting over. Even as you watch playbacks and ROTs of your work or contributions, you should be looking for specific things that you can improve on.

If you are in a role where you are judging others' performances then you will have specific criteria upon which to base those judgements, and even for you the concept of talent will remain often just that – a concept. Your concerns will no doubt be with more concrete matters such as the marketability, age range, humour – even personality and likeability – of those you are judging.

Enjoying yourself

How many jobs are there where enjoying yourself is a desirable, even necessary, part of doing it well? While it is true that people work better if they like their job, as a presenter you need to take this further. Enjoying it will help you establish a good relationship with your audience, and facilitate the smooth transfer of information from you to them. Enjoying it is infectious: if you do, the audience will.

Of course this sounds inappropriate for news and current affairs where you are dealing with death, destruction, political turmoil – more often than not bad news stories. Nevertheless news presenters certainly enjoy the sound of their own voices, and I would encourage them to do so because it will help them to get the information across all the more effectively. The adrenaline coursing through their system will not only keep them on their toes but make them high. By the same token it takes time to come down afterwards, and if you are around presenters who have just come off air you will notice their heightened state – you can feel the glow.

Think active. Do rather than be

I have noticed a tendency that some (usually but not exclusively younger trainees) who seek presentation training do not sufficiently appreciate the need to *do* something to get in front of the microphone or camera, rather than just *be* something. This tendency is fuelled by the anointing of participants in reality TV shows with celebrity status. I do not discount their appeal, and the size of audience and success of such shows is testimony to this. However as a model for those who seek success in this business this kind of media exposure is unhelpful, since the producers of such programmes are picking participants using criteria that do not necessarily apply to presenters and their guests. Take the ability to provocatively interact with others for instance; as a quality I would not deny this can be useful in front of the camera but *not on its own*.

It is a controversial issue since those who have found recognition through reality TV sometimes do go on to appear frequently in the media. But will they last if they have little to say of interest, or what they do say is offensive and/or uninformed? Even bigoted 'shock jocks', who also provocatively interact, have an expertise. Their offerings are usually of interest (to some), informed and, although may offend some, will be 'legalled' (passed by media lawyers).

TRAINING

To train or not to train

Many presenters have never had any presentation training, are proud of the fact, and are none the worse as performers for the lack of it. Some, like journalists, are suspicious of any formal training, and feel that there is no substitute for learning on the job. I understand this point of view inasmuch as more is learned on the job than in a training session, but the opportunities to a get a good presenting job to learn on are obviously limited because, perhaps like aircraft passengers, listeners and producers would prefer to have an experienced hand at the helm.

Is training any good?

I would not, however, be in this business if I did not believe in *good* training; the italics are mine and intended, since there is a lot of training on offer and you need to be wary. One rule of thumb worth applying is that if a training course is too easy to get on to, and there is no vetting of entrants, then it is probably of limited value. Sometimes independent studios with equipment and personnel which are not being used for a day or two, offer training, but at a price. You are basically paying for the hire of the personnel and equipment probably at a discount (for they are expensive). Be sure to check out the credentials of the trainers and what exactly they are offering. Often they offer show reels – see below.

Good training should be specific to your needs and specialities. For this reason one-to-one training is useful since no two presenters are alike in their needs. However, training in a group has the advantage of peer evaluation, and small group exercises with mock-up scenarios can be useful, allowing you to be producer as well as presenter, interviewee as well as interviewer, giving you useful insights into these other roles.

As a trainer I have found that each session is different because it has to be customised to every trainee's needs, even if the session follows a set pattern. Not only are people's abilities different but also their expression is unique, necessarily, and must be evaluated and coaxed individually. Confidence is important and there is a need to create a supportive atmosphere so that the trainee can be encouraged to try things out and take risks. You must be able to feel you can ask for specific attention to your individual needs from your trainer. Make sure you are suitably prepared to get the most out of any training course.

Courses

There are a limited number of good post-graduate broadcast journalism courses where the staff come from the industry and sometimes still work in it, since so many journalists and presenters are freelance. These courses also provide you with the opportunity of working attachments, or work experience at radio and TV stations, which can lead to employment opportunities. These courses have strict admissions policies which of course also contribute to their value as training vehicles.

There are also the wider-ranging media courses offered at undergraduate level. Study the prospectuses to see what facilities they have, what options the courses offer and see who in the media has been there and benefited in their career. These courses admit students on the same principles as other undergraduate courses.

Short radio and TV courses are often advertised in the trade press. Again make sure you know exactly what they are offering for the money, what their facilities are like and check the credentials of the training staff.

Adult education colleges run media courses. The fees will be very reasonable since they are subsidised. But their budgets are very limited and so equipment and facilities will be modest. The tutors usually come from the industry.

Training for guests and interviewees

If you want to polish your performance and be better able to face journalists and the media, if for instance you are in a sensitive professional area and are often called upon to defend or explain your company's policy or product, or are an expert called on to comment by the media, then you can get professional help. This is sometimes called Media Training, and covers some of what has already been discussed in this book (especially in the chapter on being interviewed).

As poachers turned gamekeepers some journalists will offer training to show what journalists want and how they get it. As their 'prey' you will be shown how to deal with the press and media to best represent your viewpoint or to show your policy/product to advantage.

Presentation training will help you relax in front of the media and show you how best to express yourself, both in content and as a performer. This book offers this. But it can also be found via the Internet from companies and individuals who specialise in such training, as I do.

Feedback

When I moved from acting to journalism and presenting I was struck by the lack of feedback I got in the latter. I would come off air and expect the sort of feedback I was used to getting coming off stage. But I was generally greeted with puzzlement that I had even asked for it. I quickly learned that it is not something to expect because colleagues do not work in a culture where it is the norm, and therefore do not generally know how to give it.

There are post-programme reviews of the editorial content, the script, and in general what worked well or less so, but often no 'notes' for the presenter. That is not to say people do not have opinions on the presenter's performance – they are just not encouraged to offer them. I learned, as presenters do, to become my own judge. But I understand that feeling of being starved of feedback. It can be remedied if you are able to consult trusted colleagues, informed audience members or presentation trainers.

But beware. In spite of what I say above there are those that offer unhelpful feedback and they may be your superiors – so you have to take note. Sometimes it is critical without offering a path to improvement. It may be cryptic and confusing: one radio presenter was told by a manager: 'It sounds too television.' I tried to work out what that meant with the presenter who came to me for training, and what could be done about it. Then there are those producers who tell you to speed up or slow down to accommodate the clock. I usually politely ignore them since I know what I can get in, within the allotted time, and my obligation is to the audience first and producer second. It is paramount that the audience 'get' what I am saying, clearly and ungabbled.

I am not saying giving or taking feedback is easy especially where a presenter's ego and confidence is concerned. In general you must cultivate your own ability to critically self-judge.

EMPLOYMENT

A career path

If it were possible to say with certainty how a presenter's career path could be chartered, what progression there was from an apprenticeship to assured established performer, even how a single appearance was going to go, then we would not be talking about (the professional life of) talent – a creative.

When people ask me if they are good enough and how they are going to *get in* or *on*, I am never sure what to say. I am reticent because I do not want to deflate or to undermine confidence, which is so important in this business. But then neither can I promise success and satisfaction as that would be irresponsible.

Although there is uncertainty at every turn in this business which makes it an exciting arena to work in, hard work is rewarded. You are never just a face in front of the camera, a 'gob on a stick'; you have something to say and the success of your performance will be about how well the audience relates to what you are telling them.

Look at the careers of successful presenters and see how they differ; but they will show some common ground. Journalism, writing, acting and other media employment, for instance, may figure. But for all those who feature a common element there will be a popular screen or radio personality who found themselves there by accident.

A producer may look for an expert on a subject being covered in a programme. They may look for a specialist journalist, academic, writer, enthusiast or known expert. If it works then the expert will be asked again, which is why you often see the same faces and voices popping up on the media on certain topics (too much sometimes). Frequent appearances as a guest can turn into further use as presenter, if the 'guest' is available. Such is one 'accidental' pathway. There are also more traditional ways.

How to get in and on

Work breeds work which poses a 'catch-22': how do you get the work in the first place that leads to further employment?

One way is to get into the voluntary sector, such as:

- Community radio and TV
- Hospital radio
- Student media.

Community and hospital media are financed by grant or subscription or have charity status, and therefore usually do not pay those who work for them. Their equipment and studio facilities can be of professional standard, however, and they provide an excellent environment to gain experience. You can find the ones that operate in your area on the Internet. A look at college extra-curricular activity will uncover student ventures.

Job adverts

The trade press such as *Broadcast* magazine and the *Press Gazette*, as well as the media sections of the newspapers, advertise media jobs which occasionally include those for presenters often for local radio. The BBC has a statutory obligation to advertise its vacancies publicly, although within the BBC staff move around on an attachment system whereby some vacancies are filled only by existing staff for a fixed term (typically six to nine months). Presenters, however, are often freelance and therefore not part of BBC staff.

BBC network radio continuity announcers and newsreaders are a mixture of staff, contract and freelance personnel recruited from both within and outside the BBC. At the time of writing the BBC TV continuity presentation team are part of Red Bee Media which looks after the broadcast operations of not only of the BBC but those of other channels as well. They employ announcers and hire voices for promotions. You will sometimes see these jobs advertised. It is worth looking at the websites (of channels, private media organisations, stations, etc.) and searching recruitment/jobs/careers for further information.

Agents

As with actors, writers and other 'talent', presenters are represented by agents who negotiate fees (for a percentage), promote, arguably find work and professionally 'represent' their clients. Their services are useful if you are busy and in demand. If you find your own work and negotiate your own fees, then you might be of less use to each other. If an agent finds you an interesting job that you like, pays well and furthers your career, then they would certainly earn their percentage. Agents are listed in directories.

Advertising

There are directories in which you can advertise and post a photo with your credits and specialities. *Spotlight* for instance, which is the industry-standard directory for actors, has a section for presenters. Some directories are more established than others and as with agents a web search brings up a lot of sites offering service. It is as well to be wary and it might be an idea to find out what sites producers and hirers really use. Nevertheless it is wise to have your face and voice available for would-be employers, and perhaps the most efficient way of doing that is to create your own website with photos, information, audio and video examples of your work. Look at the websites of the competition to see if you feel you need one. They will also be a source of ideas. And remember to update it if you want it to keep working for you. You can have links from and to it from other work-giving organisations.

Show reels

Unless you are in permanent employment, and not looking for work, it would seem advisable to have something that shows what you look and/or sound like. You can include work already broadcast as long as it is reasonably recent. You can put dedicated material on it which shows you off to advantage. You can take the advice of professionals who put show reels together for a fee. Sometimes this service is offered as part of a training package, which will include providing material, studio and equipment hire, recording and editing. It would be advisable however to think about and prepare your material, rather than necessarily accept all theirs.

Show reels, whether audio or video, should be short since casters and producers do not have a lot of time if viewing many show reels, and may only look or listen to the first minute or so. Make sure therefore that you get your strong points up front.

Job interviews, auditions

Once they have seen or heard your show reel, looked at your website, called your agent, looked you up in the directory, or seen or heard you on air, what happens if they want to see you for a job? You already have a lot going for you since they have narrowed the field down to a short list and you are on it. Well done. Do not mess it up with lack of research. Make sure you know everything you can about their operation, and impress them with your interest and knowledge. Enthusiasm, ideas and perhaps an indefinable chemistry should see you over the line. If the competition is stiff and you do not manage to get the job, then maybe one of the other contenders had more of the latter – make sure you had more of the former two and that the ideas are appropriate.

I knew a performer who went for an audition/interview for a job where he thought they were looking for a comedian. He went in, cracked a few jokes and was full of beans –'larging' it. He knew something was afoot when he noticed the solemn faces of the producers. When they finally spoke to welcome him and to ask him what qualities he thought he had to present this programme about bereavement, he said: 'Can I go out and come in again?'

'AND THAT BRINGS US TO THE...

...end of the programme but before I go a final word...'

Programming, networks, platforms, technology and the market all change, and that makes useful commentary on them all too rapidly obsolete. It is only right that fashions governing presentation will change, and whether one approves or not of certain innovations is hardly important in the face of market realities. Nevertheless it is worth asking if there are enduring presentation qualities which can be possessed, learned and appreciated which transcend the reality of relentless media trends. I have made it my mission to define some qualities which will work for you, whatever the platform, programme, channel or market. The proof of improvement is easily measured: you can simply see or hear it on playback.

However as with most creative endeavours there is a certain important part – a gift if you like – that comes from leftfield, while your focus is elsewhere. It is unlooked for, surprises you, but which you will, with practice and sensitivity, recognise as valid. Most creative output, although meticulously planned, must allow for this possibility. Looking back on successful programmes, a certain important element seems often to have come this way: *as if* by accident. I would allow here for some luck too. But also remember that it would not have come at all had there not been hard work, preparation and focus in the first place.

SUMMARY

1. Be a team player. Enjoy yourself and *do* rather than *be*.
2. Decide what training you need and look carefully at what is on offer, and the credentials of the trainers.
3. As presenter or guest look for valuable feedback from professionals.
4. Career paths are not conventional. Websites, ads, agents and directories can help. Subsidised media outlets can get you started.
5. Don't forget to allow for some magic ingredient to lift your well prepared work.

Glossary

Broadcast copy: text written for broadcast.

Cans: headphones.

Coming out: ending a broadcast or recording.

Doughnut: interview of several interviewees in turn with linking material between as if in a circle.

Dubbing or **dubbing off:** copying/recording already recorded material.

Early out: optional ending before the end.

Fader: the sliding volume control on a radio/audio desk which will 'open' or close an audio channel including the microphone.

Fluff: stumbling over a word when reading/broadcasting.

Gallery: control room for a video/TV broadcast in a studio. Director, vision mixer, and other technicians as well as producer or editor control the programme from here.

Howl-round: an ugly, high-pitched noise, resulting from having mic and speakers open at the same time.

Idents: reference to the identity of the station (station ident) or programme (programme ident). For example: 'You're listening to "Radio Star". This is "Afternoon Jazz".'

Legaled: scrutinised by lawyers for libel or defamation.

Lip-mic: hand-held mic with a ridge at the top so that you can speak right into it.

Name check: saying your name on air: 'You're listening to the Breakfast Show with me Alec Sabin.'

OB: outside broadcast.

OOV: out of vision.

Podcasts: audio scripts recorded to be downloaded to an MP3 player ('pod') via the Internet. Increasingly with video. Often download as episodes, so that the 'subscriber' can have them automatically downloaded, for later transfer to the pod.

Popping: occurs when you make plosive sounds (e.g. *p*'s and *b*'s). These sounds produce a magnified 'pop'.

Pot (cut): ending before the end – an earlier (and optional) finish in a longer broadcast text or other material.

Pre-fade: (radio) a sound source (typically music or signature tune) on a channel not faded up until needed which is usually when the presenter/announcer has stopped talking – it is sometimes faded up over the closing words of the presenter. It is often timed to finish precisely at a pre-arranged point (e.g. the end of the programme).

Print copy: text written for print media (newspapers and magazines).

PTC: piece to camera.

ROT: recording off transmission or off air.

RP: received pronunciation. So-called standard English pronunciation seemingly without regional accent.

Segue: (sometimes written **segue-way**): the junction or joining of two pieces of information, text, music/text on air attempting the seamless.

Self-op: one person operating the equipment and presenting.

Shock jocks: from US radio mainly, presenters (disc jockeys – hence 'jock') who provoke the audience and phone-in guests with extreme views sometimes featuring rude/racist/homophobic/misogynist/obscene/often right-wing statements, stimulating discussion and/or further extreme reaction.

Throw: from one presenter to another – or from anchor to reporter – 'Jim Smith, what's the latest?'

Time check: as 'name check' but with the time.

Two-way or **Q & A:** one journalist/presenter interviewing another – usually with pre-arranged questions.

Vox pop: voice of the people. The reporter/journalist interviews several members of the general public and makes a collage of their responses to questions on a single issue, or to a single question, to give a flavour of different opinions on the issue.

Webcasts: presentations by video or audio via the Internet, sometimes including voice-over to film.

Wild track: recording a track of background noise for editing purposes. Especially necessary for recording interviews in a noisy environment or outside where there is ambient sound.

Wrap: finish, ending.

Bibliography and useful contacts

Bibliography

Media and broadcast presentation

Robert McLeish, *Radio Production*, Focal Press, Oxford, 2003.

Jenni Mills, *The Broadcast Voice*, Focal Press, Oxford, 2004.

Janet Trewin, *Presenting on TV and Radio*, Focal Press, Oxford, 2004.

Ann S. Utterback, *Broadcast Voice Handbook*, Bonus Books, Chicago, 2004.

Voice

Cicely Berry, *Your Voice and How to Use it*, Virgin Books, London, 2000.

Anne Karpf, *The Human Voice*, Bloomsbury, London, 2007.

Richard Payne, *Vocal Skills*, Management Pocketbooks, Alresford, 2004.

Patsy Rodenburg, *The Right to Speak*, Methuen, London, 1992.

Bernard Graham Shaw, *Voice Overs: A Practical Guide*, A & C Black, London, 2000.

J. Clifford Turner, *Voice and Speech in the Theatre*, Pitman, London, 1970.

Training

Kat Koppett, *Training Using Drama*, Kogan Page, London, 2002.

Presentation

Andrew Bradbury, *Successful Presentation Skills*, Kogan Page London, 2002.

Libby Hammond, *Is There a Speaker in the Room?* Management Books, Cirencester, 2003.

Dorothy Leeds, *Power Speak*, Career Press, Franklin Lakes, NJ, 2003.

Andrew Leigh and Michael Maynard, *Perfect Presentation*, Random House, London, 2003.

Sean Misteil, *The Communicator's Pocketbook*, Management Pocketbooks, Alresford, 2001.

Richard Olivier and Nichols Janni, *Peak Performance Presentations*, Spiro Press, London, 1998.

Cristina Stuart, *Effective Speaking*, Pan Books, London, 1998.

Journalism and law

L.C.J. McNae, *Essential Law for Journalists*, Butterworths, London, 1982.

Websites

www.alecsabin.com My own website with updates and useful information and advice. How to contact me. And how to book training.

www.bbc.co.uk The BBC website for all news and information about the BBC.

www.bjtc.org.uk Broadcast Journalism Training Council – invaluable information for training and accredited courses.

www.radioacademy.org UK radio information.

www.radiocentre.org UK commercial radio information.

www.skillset.org UK creative media help and information for professionals.

www.ucas.com Undergraduate course search.

www.postgrad.hobsons.com Postgraduate course search.

www.nuj.org.uk National Union of Journalists.

For media training and short TV and radio presentation courses any search will bring up a choice of options.

Index

Notes